A
FANCY
DINNER PARTY

*With a foreword by
Jonathan Maberry*

EDITED BY
HILARY COMFORT

Published by Grey Gecko Press, Katy, Texas.

www.greygeckopress.com

Printed in the United States of America

Design by Grey Gecko Press

Library of Congress Cataloging-in-Publication Data

Kristopher, Jason et al.

A fancy dinner party / Jason Kristopher et al; [edited by] Hilary Comfort

Library of Congress Control Number: 2012937515

ISBN 978-0-9836185-9-1

10 9 8 7 6 5 4 3 2 1

First Edition

*For all the new and still-struggling authors
whose stories have yet to be told.*

A Fancy Dinner Party
Menu

Appetizers

The Finger of Death
Gabrielle Alan

Being Bad
H.C.H. Ritz

Civility
Lee Lackey

Salads

Misty Mountain Morning
Leo King

The Faithful Farmers
B.H. Werner

Entrees

Hybrid
Austin Malone

A Fancy Dinner Party
Leo King

Heirloom
B.H. Werner

Desserts

Peace Meal
Wayne Basta

Miss Tilly
Amy Theacasi

Cheese

The Art of Steaming
Jason Kristopher

The Arrangement
George Wright Padgett

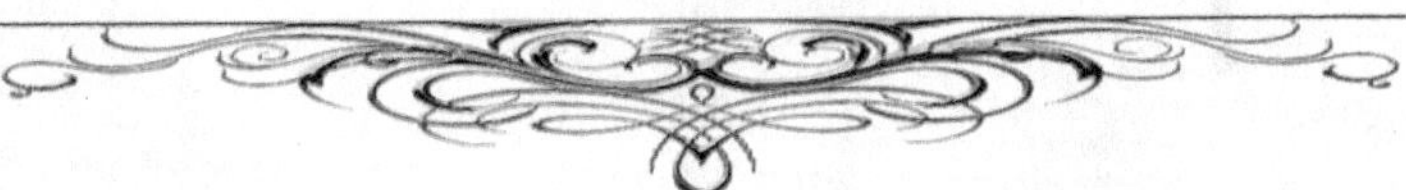

Foreword

Jonathan Maberry

So . . . okay, cannibalism.

In the horror game, we tend to cover a lot of odd topics. Mass slaughter. Hordes of the living dead. Pasty-faced eastern-European noblemen in tuxedos with a taste for hemoglobin. Titanic fire-breathing lizards stomping their way through Asian cities. Demons and ghosts. Shapeshifters and mummies. And even very human monsters like Gary Heidnik and Hannibal Lecter.

Horror subject matter is, well, horrifying. Occasionally disgusting. Often disturbing. And scary as hell.

But nothing provokes a more profound and atavistic dread than the consuming of human flesh. It's the ultimate taboo, the one line that we tell ourselves we would never—*could never*—cross.

Unless . . .

Unless our plane crashes on a snowy mountaintop and all those dead fellow passengers are just *lying* there.

Unless you're born into one of those cultures in present-day tropical Africa, or in remote spots in Melanesia, or the Korowai tribe, where eating human flesh is part of required cultural practice. Hell, the glorious tropical paradise of Fiji was once known as the Cannibal Islands.

There's even a theory that Neanderthals were cannibals (hence the paucity of complete skeletons found), and a related theory that our modern ancestors may have dined on the Neanderthals. We even have a cool scientific name for it: anthropophagy.

But still . . . eww! For most of us, when we think of cannibals, we think of Jeffrey Dahmer and Albert Fish.

Modern man is not comfortable with the idea. Perhaps it's because we've grown out of it. Or we've been guilted out of it by clerics and lawmakers who have labeled it as sinful and wrong. Or maybe we just lost the taste for it. It doesn't, I am reliably told, taste like chicken.

But damn if we don't enjoy spinning yarns about it! We see it in movies—*Texas Chainsaw Massacre* to *Silence of the Lambs* to *The Road.* We see it on TV in *Buffy the Vampire Slayer* and *The X-Files* and even on *It's Always Sunny in Philadelphia.* And we write a lot of stories about it. *American Psycho*, Charlie Higson's *The Enemy*, Poppy Z. Brite's *Exquisite Corpse*, and even a reference in *The Hunger Games.* Not to mention the entirety of zombie literature.

Which brings us to *A Fancy Dinner Party.* This is a collection of very odd, highly weird, and completely delicious little tales that have only one thing in common. Some part of the human body will, inevitably, be consumed.

Mmmm. Mouth-watering, isn't it?

Sit back, tuck in your napkin, keep your favorite steak sauce handy, and dig into this bizarre feast. It's a menu you won't soon forget.

Bon Appétit.

Jonathan Maberry

The Finger of Death

Gabrielle Alan

The taste of one's own flesh should be unpleasant.

Daetric finds it spongy, tough, and slightly salty from sweat, which is the only indication of his nerves. The already severed skin at the base of the ring makes it easy to slip his teeth in and pull. The skin is pliable, easy for him to sink his teeth into; the difficulty is tearing. Once he rips a strip free, blood streams from the wound, and he sucks it down, his mouth sealed on the finger. He doesn't want to make a mess.

The pain is within his threshold; he breathes through his nose evenly, and focuses on why he is here. As long as he can remember that, he can withstand any trial or tribulation that may come.

One of his canines scrapes roughly against the metal ring secured on his forefinger, sending a tremor down his spine. He resolves to be more careful, and he gingerly eats around the ring.

A bead of sweat gathers at his temple and falls, trickling down his bare chest and thigh. Circled about him are the rest of the Order; the shrouded figures only remind Daetric further of his nakedness.

"It's symbolic," Adept Tarek had explained on one of their many walks during the last three years of his initiation. "When you are born, you come into this world nude and new. This will be your rebirth into our Order. You must be bare to receive the blessing."

Daetric had nodded.

"There is one other thing." Adept Tarek had held up his hand, tugging the glove off, revealing his Death Finger. It was devoid of skin and muscle, held together through magic and the *Santric* ring it bore.

"You must also make the sacrifice. The method you choose will dictate the faction you belong to, and you will go to join that Order."

"I am ready, Adept, whatever my choices."

"I have a feeling, dear boy, you will choose the most difficult path."

And he did. At the beginning of the ceremony, Adept Tarek towered over him as he was given his options, laid out on a plank between them.

"Now is your choice. First: by my hand." He indicated a knife, the handle made of finger bones, its blade black with rivets of red. This would be the quickest method. "By theirs." He gestured toward a pot of flesh-eating insects, which would be the slowest method. "Or by your own means." He held his hands out towards Daetric.

Daetric met his mentor's eyes. "I choose my own means."

Tarek nodded and lifted a finger, and the plank was removed.

"Daetric has made his decision," Tarek announced to the assembled men. "By his own means, he shall join this Order." He twisted his *Santric* ring, working it off his forefinger, his mouth a grim line, with only a slight twitch of pain in the corner. Once it was free, he slipped the ring onto Daetric's finger.

It took all of Daetric's training and stubborn stoicism to keep his face stone and his knees from trembling. Even as it tightened, pressing deeper and deeper, constricting blood to the finger — even as it cut into the skin, severing veins and muscles, stanching the blood flow, and then melting the skin below, until it was just the warm metal against the bone – even then, he kept his face still.

As he works his way to the knuckle, nibbling at stray strands of muscles, he lifts his eyes in search of his mentor. But Adept Tarek fades into the sea of shadow cloaks, all with their hoods pulled down.

Death Fingers point at him, some a dull phlegm yellow edged in brown through age, others gleaming white in the firelight. The old hands, and new, in this trade of death. In the low light, their fingers remind him of twigs.

Aeron used to tie a twig to his own finger, when they played Keeper of the Peace in the woods behind their farm. Aeron would be Justice, and Jaemin would be the Evildoer, and the rest of the children — Raelin, Gaeml, and Daetric — would be the victims.

Jaemin, the Evildoer, would spin a wild tale about all the cruelty he would do, his brown eyes dancing and his face twisting into smirks and sneers. And the younger siblings would run into the woods and hide, hoping the Evildoer would be caught before he found them.

Gabrielle Alan

If Aeron, Justice, caught the Evildoer and poked him without anyone seeing, he would win, ending the reign of tyranny. If the Evildoer found all of the others first, he would win.

But sometimes, Jaemin would find everyone except Daetric, and Aeron wouldn't be able to get Jaemin without anyone seeing, either. Eventually, Aeron would give up and declare Jaemin the winner.

And only then would Daetric come out. It was during these times that Daetric would privately declare himself the winner. He was always the best hider.

It's why he survived.

It was dark, and Aeron was shaking him and Gaeml. Jaemin stood at the foot of the bed, holding Raelin's hand.

"Want to play Keeper?" Aeron asked.

Gaeml squinted up at his brother. "But the wolves are out."

"We'll play inside."

They never played inside.

"Where's Father and Mother?" Raelin asked. Under one arm was the doll Father had crafted for her. Mother had been trying to stop her from sleeping with it now that she was ten winters old.

"They're playing too, Rae," Aeron said. "They are going to be the Evildoers. They're outside, counting. Jae and I are both going to be Justice. How does that sound?"

"Wait." Daetric reached under his pillow, pulling out string and some twigs. "You need Death Fingers."

"That's right, Dae, we do." Aeron held out his finger.

Above all about that night, Daetric remembered Aeron's fingers trembling as he tied the twig on his brother's finger.

As Daetric makes his way past the second knuckle, the skin is closer to the bone, harder to catch between his teeth. He moves his finger to the side of his mouth and begins to gnaw.

Daetric darted from his room before anyone else. He knew where to hide. He'd been cleaning the fire pit earlier in the week, and he had heard a sound up the chimney. Looking up, he'd seen a bird make its way up and out the chute. How did it get there? he wondered. He easily found places for his hands and feet in the stone as he climbed just a little way up. There he discovered a cubby, where one roof beam had been cut too short; inside was a half-built nest. He crawled in, and to his delight, he could look out through the paneling to the main room.

Daetric spied his brothers, standing in the front room; they stood side by side. Both looked more like Father than ever, despite being only ten and three winters. Then Aeron placed three fingers over his heart and bowed his head. Jaemin followed suit. Why were they praying? That was when Daetric knew this wasn't a game.

Shouting came from outside, and then the clash of steel and a woman's cry. Aeron pulled two of Father's swords from the wall and handed one to Jaemin.

The door shattered; a burly man strode in, blood dripping from his sword. On one side of his head hung a half a dozen or so bones that clicked together with eve-

Gabrielle Alan

ry step. They were of different lengths, but all were narrow, and at the bases were black rings.

Aeron and Jaemin swung clumsily at the man. Their
thin arms could barely lift their swords, and each swing
was slow and easily deflected. The man laughed as each
blow became slower. Finally, he knocked Jaemin to the
floor and buried his sword in his stomach.

Aeron let out a howl and slashed his sword, catching the man by surprise and slicing his face from
eyebrow to chin.

The man roared and brought his sword across
Aeron's throat.

A cry sounded from across the room. It was Gaeml.
He was always so restless and curious. He must have
heard the fight and come to investigate. He charged at
the man with his wooden practice sword.

Daetric shut his eyes and stuffed his hand in his
mouth and bit down as hard as he could. He didn't want
the man to hear him, nor did he want to see any more of
his family die.

He could hear the man stalking through the house;
he knew from the shrieks when he found Rae. And he
knew from the silence when she was dead.

He stayed there for hours, watching that man sit on
his father's chair and eat his family's food. The bodies of
his siblings lay at his feet.

Daetric may have dozed at some point, but he
jerked awake at the sound of voices.

"So, I take it, they were against selling?" The new
man's back was to the chimney. He had on a long fur
cloak with a hood. Daetric strained his neck trying to
catch a glimpse of his face.

The burly man slurped from the cup. "Correct."

Gabrielle Alan

"Did you kill them all?"

"Yes."

"What a shame. That means there is no one to inherit this land."

"I suppose it goes to the crown, then."

"I suppose so." The man in the cloak pulled a coin purse out of his pocket and tossed it on the table. "Your fee."

And then he was gone.

The past ten years have led to this moment. No longer is he that helpless child in that cramped space. He is a man, and soon will be an apprentice in this order. The gods will grant him the power to take a life with one touch. He will wield the power of justice and strike down the evil and the corrupt.

For five hundred years, the Order of Shadow Knights have been tasked with keeping the five kingdoms at peace. They bend the knee to no king; they are an impartial observer until needed. Now he, too, will don a shadow cloak and learn the art of being an assassin.

Daetric tears the last bit of flesh from the pad of his finger. He chews slowly, savoring, then swallows.

The taste of one's own flesh should be unpleasant. But as the power rolls through him, seeping into his pores and then down into his very bones, it is anything but.

Gabrielle Alan

Being Bad

A Story from the New America

H. C. H. Ritz

He was going to have to kill his best friend's daughter, and he really didn't want to.

They stood a dozen paces from each other on a rooftop. She was pointing a gun at him — his own gun. She swayed back and forth, holding the weapon unsteadily with one hand and holding back her long hair with the other. She was crying, her nose and eyes red.

"You're not real! You're not real, because if you're real, then you're in my head, and you *can't* be in my head." She took a deep breath and screamed at him, as if the words alone could make him vanish in a puff of smoke, "You can't be real anymore!"

The grizzled old man didn't really see the gun as a threat. He didn't think she would use it. All he could see was how young and innocent she was, and how hopeless it seemed now that he realized how badly they'd damaged her.

The agents of the Domestic Awareness Agency would be right behind them, he knew. And he couldn't afford to wait around until they caught up. If he let her delay them, they'd both die.

Wayne Webster Watts was not about dying. He didn't mind taking chances, but his second book — illegally published in the secret underground, just like his first one — was titled *9 Lives* for a reason.

Moments like these, phrases he'd written popped randomly into his head. "Don't try to take away my boxing match..."

The girl was a mess, but he wasn't seeing too straight himself. The years of copious drug and alcohol abuse in the underground, never mind all of the head trauma from all of the illegal fights he'd been in, had caught up to him in the last couple of years. It was a miracle he'd managed to get her out of the DAA's prison and get them both this far. His vision kept blurring, and he wiped his eyes.

The girl shot at him and missed.

He jumped about half a mile. "Dammit, girl! Don't do that!"

"You can't be real!" she sobbed.

Being shot at was good, in a way. It reminded him that what was happening was real and not a memory of something held safely in the past; he'd been having trouble telling the difference sometimes. He felt more in touch now.

He stepped toward her, placating. "Bree, you can't shoot me, okay? It's fine, I don't have to be real. I can be imaginary. I don't mind."

Wailing, she clamped both hands over her ears. "No... you can't be in my head... it isn't safe... I can't have... what isn't good... in here *anymore*."

Tears came to the old man's eyes. He'd thought he was beyond all that by now, but this whole situation went straight to his heart. He'd seen a little girl grow up to be the young woman standing in front of him, and now she was irretrievably broken by what they'd done to her in prison.

No woman in the secret underground had a long life expectancy — living in near-anarchy was just too harsh

— but this just wasn't right. She was too young. And she shouldn't be broken like this; dead would be better.

She was right, he wasn't *good*... but dammit, he *ought* to have a place in Bree's head. He'd earned it, hadn't he? He'd helped teach her how to stay safe in the underground all these years. Anyway, he'd tried.

He took a few cautious steps toward her. He put up his hands. "Bree, it's okay. I'm *not* real, and I'm not in your head, either, okay? And anyway, I'll be gone in just a minute. I promise." He nearly choked on his promise. He'd be gone from her mind because he'd have killed her. But he had no choice — it was too late to help her in any other way.

He took another few steps toward her. Just as he got close enough to reach for the gun, he saw her face change. The set of her jaw, the insanity shining in her eyes, warned him that she was about to shoot him for real. As she brought the gun toward his face, he slapped it from her hand.

He dove for the weapon, grunting loudly as he hit the ground; his graceful years were over. He came up in a roll anyway, weapon in hand. He pointed it at Bree.

She just looked at him helplessly, crying softly and hiccupping, her long hair tossed by the wind.

Finally, he realized that he couldn't bring himself to pull the trigger. Despite what common sense told him, he still had to hope that she could get better.

Instead, he got up and hit her in the head with the butt of the pistol. She fell instantly, and he winced. He knelt and checked her eyes and pulse to make sure he hadn't killed her by accident. Then he heard shouting from behind him. He was out of time.

H. C. H. Ritz

He picked her up and maneuvered her into place over his shoulder, despite the distracting complaints from his lower back.

His vision blurred again, and he swiped his hand over his face. He stood up confused, the weight of Bree's unconscious body somehow gone from his shoulder. He'd lost track of time again. Now he was in a dark tunnel in the underground, and they were behind him, shouting.

He ran. He had a flashlight in his hand, which he was using to reveal the path in front of him. He couldn't remember what he'd been doing a minute ago, or where Bree had disappeared to. But the DAA was right behind him. He could only hope they weren't packing their dust guns, which would disintegrate him in mid-stride if they found their target.

A few frantic steps later, he remembered his strategy. Of course. He always had a plan. He liked risk-taking, but he wasn't crazy. Well, not until more recently.

He led the way through a specific left turn — he'd marked the spot a few hours ago with blue chalk. He glanced back to make sure they hadn't turned the corner and couldn't see him as he slowed down and chose his steps carefully. His flashlight reflected off the large puddle of water covering almost the entire hallway, except for where he stepped along the side. Glancing up, he made sure the wires were still dangling down from the overhead lighting into the puddle.

He found the inline switch he'd installed in one of the wires on the other side of the water, and now he just had to wait. He shut off his flashlight.

Moments later, the men charged into the hallway, splashing into the puddles. He flipped the switch, and a brilliant pattern of light erupted in the tunnel as he electrocuted the lot of them. He left the switch engaged until he saw smoke rising from their still bodies.

He didn't smell anything. That seemed odd. He thought he remembered smelling an awful cooking meat odor before...

Before? *What* before?

He flipped off the switch and the light show stopped. Steam rose from the puddles of water. Now he was very tired, and he couldn't remember what he'd been thinking about a minute ago. He squatted down in the darkness to rest for a moment.

The moans of dying men drifted out of the darkness, but they didn't bother him. On the one hand, everything was feeling a bit muted anyway, like he had the volume down too low on a wallscreen that was too far away. On the other, death was nothing new to him anyway. Another quote from his second book came to him: "There's nothing like a conversation with a corpse..."

He was dizzy. Too much hard running for an old man. He closed his eyes.

He was grateful to feel the warmth of the fire, soon after. He heard soft sobbing along with the crackling of the flames and opened his eyes. He didn't remember starting the fire in the fireplace or putting Bree in the cage in this room, deep in his living quarters in the underground, but it made sense that he would have.

Everything was feeling normal again — the volume turned back up. He felt more at ease.

He went over to her. She was on her knees, hanging from the bars, weeping.

"Honey," he said softly. "It's going to be okay." He squatted down and reached through the bars to stroke her hair, but she jerked away.

H. C. H. Ritz

He settled down on his haunches, looking at her. It tore at him to see her this way.

"We'll help you, honey," he said. "Somehow."

"You don't understand," she whispered, her voice shaky. "I'm bad. I'm a bad person. I have to start over. I can't be this person anymore."

"Naw," he said, waving the idea away. Inside, he wanted to laugh. Good and bad meant nothing in the underground. That was the whole *point* of the underground and its delicious anarchy — it was nothing like the picture-perfect New America up top.

"I've done terrible things," she said hoarsely. Her eyes glinted in the firelight.

"Bree, we all do bad things." He had just electrocuted half a dozen men, hadn't he?

Alarm bells rang in his mind. Something seemed wrong about the memory. Looking back now, he realized that it was an *old* memory. That hadn't even been the DAA, it had been the Double Double Gang. And it had all happened a few years back. No, *more* than a few years back. He'd written about it in his first book.

Then how had he gotten the two of them away from the DAA just now?

He shook his head as if to clear the cobwebs, trying to summon up the memory of what had really happened, but it didn't work. The memories just weren't there right now. He felt defeated by the tricks of his own deteriorating mind. He rubbed his face wearily and turned his attention back to Bree and her predicament.

He thought of a quote from his second book, and told it to Bree. "Good and bad is a refuge of the weak. For the strong, just doing is all that matters." Even if he could no longer *remember* what he'd done...

H. C. H. Ritz

The young woman shook her head. "I... you don't understand..."

"Bree," he said firmly, "you can't have done anything worse than *I've* ever done. Okay? I *know* you. You're a pretty good kid, all things considered."

Bree swallowed and started sobbing quietly. "I.... I ate a... I ate..." She finished too softly for him to hear.

"What?" He leaned in closer to the cage.

"I ate *babies*." Her voice turned to a wail.

He rocked back on his heels. "Naw," he said. He couldn't believe that. He stared at her from under his bushy eyebrows.

"I did. I did... they were still alive... I cut the flesh off their little arms *and ate it*." She finished with a note of hysteria.

"No, honey." Then he realized what had really happened. "No, the DAA gives you drugs in prison, causes you hallucinations. It - whatever you saw - it wasn't real."

"It was," she whispered. She flung herself suddenly against the wall of the cage, startling him. "You have to understand. I'm bad. You have to see that. You have to *know*. So I can start over. And then it won't be real anymore. I can *make* it not be real."

He rubbed his eyes and sighed. He got up and paced around the room, hearing her soft sobbing behind him. He felt miserably helpless, and old, and tired. His vision blurred again, and he shook it off.

"Uncle Wayne?" Her voice seemed to have changed. She sounded so sweet.

He glanced over at the cage and saw, to his surprise, that Bree was about eight years old again, somehow.

H. C. H. Ritz

She was wearing a pretty blue dress; it seemed to iridesce in the firelight. She looked so innocent. "I want to be good," she said plaintively, her face shining.

Her voice was so powerful, so clear, it seemed to resonate inside his eardrums. The color of her dress was so brilliant that it almost seemed to blind him. Even from across the room, he could see every tiny pore on her cute little nose. The very air shimmered.

Somewhere distant in his mind, alarm bells rang again. Something funny was going on... but he couldn't tell what it was. Maybe he had taken some drugs a bit ago. That was something he might do.

Either way, poor little Bree shouldn't be in that ugly cage.

He went over and unlocked it, vividly feeling the cold metal under his hands, hearing every little clink and clank of the key in the lock. It was all magnified.

She came out of the cage and took his hand, smiling up at him and making him smile, too. He felt so good, so full of love, he thought his heart might burst.

Then everything shifted. The drug-like intensity and euphoria were gone. Grown-up Bree was holding his old Army-issue knife right up to his face with a demented expression. He tried to push her away, and discovered that he was chained to the cage. His shirt was off. His heart was racing. Everything felt gritty and ugly and normal again. The sound of her breathing was harsh.

He blinked hard. Maybe... maybe this part wasn't real. He could hope, couldn't he? He could just wait and see...

"You have to know I'm bad," she said hoarsely. "You have to know. And when we *all* know, then I can start again." Her eyes filled with tears and her face twisted as she shoved the knife into his shoulder. He howled in pain and shock as she carved out a chunk of his flesh, spilling blood in warm torrents down his body. Oh, no... this was real; horribly real.

She lifted the bloody chunk of his shoulder to her lips. "I'm bad, just like they said," she whispered, and sank her teeth into his flesh.

For more about The New America, look for the novel, *The Lightbringers*, by H. C. H. Ritz, in the fall of 2012.

H. C. H. Ritz

Civility

Lee Lackey

He waited. Stranded in the dank blackness, in still water underneath stale air, he waited. The years passed, and the water slid ever lower in the cylinder of stones, while he grew weaker. Even the sky, blocked by a massive stone twenty feet overhead, could not keep him company.

In time, the land outside the well cracked from drought. The crops withered and died; weeds grew tall, just to scorch in the relentless sun. Animals abandoned their homes. Men cursed and struggled in the dry dust of their fields. He could feel the suffering, the arid soil outside his home, but he was helpless to stop it. When his bond with man had held strong, the aquifers had gushed forth, bringing life and plenty.

All had marveled at the wealth the waters brought. He had even reached into the heavens, pulled the rains from the floodplains, and wrung the clouds of their silvery drops. Now, the bond abandoned but not broken, he floated, dreaming of his forbidden birthplace in the murky depths of the sea, and of his second home in the Far East where cherry blossoms had drifted onto his stream. Before, he had always had opportunities to go forth and seek his due, if it was not voluntarily forthcoming.

But then the bond had sealed him to an outlander, a gaijin. The agreement had given him passage across the seas and through the underground rivers to this place, where he had hoped to establish a new home for himself, outside of the crowded land he'd come from.

After decades, the friendship had died, and he suffered.

At long last, a gentle scraping of stone on stone echoed down the well shaft. His thoughts interrupted, he drifted down underneath the water. With neither trust nor fear, unblinking, he watched the crescent light of the sun grow full overhead. And he waited.

"Ha-ha! It's still got water, Diane! We can have the drilling crew out next month to get running water for the house! You hear that? No more heading to your parents' house for washing and cooking!" said Ted, his green eyes glowing with excitement. His brown shirt with pearl snaps shone in the sunlight, while his jean shorts—made himself by cutting through a pair of old jeans—hung tattered against his knees.

Ted grabbed a metal bucket with a long hemp rope attached to it and threw the bucket into the well while hanging onto the other end of the rope. After a splash, he pulled the bucket up from the well. Diane waddled across the grassy yard to the red brick of the well.

She hunched her lithe frame over her bulging stomach, subconsciously protecting the baby within. Diane smiled at Ted and hugged him, her blond hair swishing around his neck.

"And not a moment too soon. I love my folks, Ted, but I love them more when I don't see them every day," said Diane.

Ted frowned and said, "What do you mean? I thought you enjoyed seeing your folks." He furrowed his broad eyebrows as he turned to Diane. "They've helped us build a new life together. They've treated us like guests at their home, even though we've visited every night for the past week!"

Lips thinning in annoyance, Diane looked toward the well. She followed the cracks in the red brick masonry jutting up from the knee-high grass. She explained, "I know, Ted, but they won't let me do anything for myself. *Sit down, Diane! Don't exert yourself, Diane! We'll take care of it, Diane!* It's infuriating! I'm pregnant, not sick!"

Ted laughed and then pulled his wife into his broad chest. He puckered his lips until he looked like a sick fish, saying in a cutesy voice, "Mah poor baby is tired of being babied for the baby. She's a big girl, she can take care of herself!" Diane pulled away, frustration wrinkling her face. She sat down on the warm brick steps leading to the house. The aimless wandering and occasional snorts of the cows in the pasture to the east soothed her a little. Strands of an electric fence ran between the pasture and yard.

To the west, an old two-story farmhouse remained silhouetted against the sun. Ted sighed and then sat down beside her. His arms formed a triangle between his knees, fingers interlaced.

"Look, darlin', I know it's been tough starting a new life out here on my parents' farm. No water, bad insulation, no company. Hell, even I've had a hard time living out here. But I'll help you through this, because there's no one I'd rather build a life with than you. And I'm sure my parents would welcome you here, if they were still alive."

Diane's tension slackened as she turned back to him. He was sweet, even when he missed the point entirely. A small peck on the lips, and Ted went back to the well. Diane loved Ted, even if his innate lack of shame embarrassed her to no end.

When he had quit his job at the bank to start over with the farm, the opportunity to live a simpler life had appealed to her. She'd quit her job as a nutritionist, hoping to spend time growing the organic food she studied. But their time on the farm had proved harder than she had expected. The irrigation ditches were choked with weeds, while the barren ground fought every planting. The troubles spread to the animals, too: cows lost to disease, pigs refusing to eat their feed, free-range chickens eaten by predators.

The old house was the least of their problems, but it loomed largest for Diane since she spent much of her time there. Besides the aforementioned lack of running water, the doors no longer sat square in their frames and couldn't be shut properly.

Instead, they had to use ropes to secure the doors— it was insecure, but any intruder that made their way to the house would break the windows anyway. A constant draft stole through the house, making it chilly at nighttime.

Diana silently watched Ted working at the well, drawing up water and playfully spilling it back into the well. His boundless energy and upbeat attitude kept him going long after others would have given up.

She even found herself loving the farm the more she worked on it. After long hours tending the house and garden, Diane believed she would do anything to keep it going.

Wind swept through the open door as Ted entered the house. Diane shivered underneath the quilt on her lap. She was reading a book on etiquette that her mother had given her. She stuck a finger in her book to hold her place and looked up.

"Did you get the cows taken care of, hon?" she said.

"Yeah, they just needed some extra mineral licks. I should have put them out this morning, but I wanted to check on that water well. You ready for dinner? I should have it done in about thirty minutes or so," said Ted.

"Yes, hon. I'll be hungry then," said Diane, diving back into her book.

Various farm implements lined the walls, lending a utilitarian air to the room. An axe and scythe crossed each other on the far side of the room like a peasant's coat of arms. They were both in good repair, since Diane had spent several nights fixing them.

As Diane read, something tickled the edge of her vision, and she looked outside. The night was still, the brick path that led to the gravel road shining like a thread in the darkness. The full moon illuminated the front yard from the old well to the electric fence, but Diane's eyes had trouble adjusting from the brightness of the lamp beside her.

Diane scanned the grass, trying to find something wrong. She finally settled on the old well that Ted had uncovered that morning. It took her a few seconds to notice that a dark shape covered the right side of the well. Her heart raced for a few moments, and she nearly called for Ted.

But Diane couldn't determine if the mass was a shadow or an animal. It certainly didn't look like any animal she knew. Diane moved her head around to view the well from different angles. She finally decided the dark spot was just a shadow and opened her book again.

Lee Lackey

She shivered as she turned the pages, the cold of the night seeping in through the windows on either side of her. The wooden walls didn't hold in much heat, either.

Surprisingly, a fog now covered the yard outside, and moisture rolled in, forming droplets on the windows. The farm had been bone dry since the couple arrived. Now, the rug under Diane's feet contained a dampness that sucked the heat out of her bones. Even the air felt like clammy syrup; the cold evaporated the strength from Diane's muscles. She shivered, but she felt grateful for the water now settling on the ground.

Diane crossed the wood plank floor to the brick fireplace, which had firewood stacked beside it. She picked up a couple of logs and threw them in. She had almost finished when Ted surprised her by gently restraining her arm.

"Now stop that, darling. We can't have you straining yourself, or you might hurt the baby!" said Ted.

"I can take care of it. I was cold and didn't want to slow down dinner." Diane tightened her eyebrows in exasperation. Ted's chivalry was one of his best qualities, but it could also annoy her to no end.

"Late dinner is better than you hurting yourself. Why don't you go sit down? I'll take care of it." Ted butted in between Diane and the fireplace. He proceeded to grab a starter log and place it next to the woodpile Diane had made.

Diane grumbled, "I already did most of the work," and went back to the chair to wait. Ted fiddled with the fireplace for thirty minutes, but he couldn't get any of the wood to light. He mumbled and grimaced and shook his head as match after match failed to start a flame. Finally, he gave up and went back to preparing dinner. Diane huddled deeper underneath her quilt.

Lee Lackey

Above the fireplace, a sepia-toned photograph of Ted's grandfather smiled down. Ted had told her that the photo came after his grandpa's service in World War II, when his hand had already been amputated. According to Ted's story, medical service had not yet been set up in Japan when his grandfather's hand had become infected. A surgeon for the former Japanese Army had cut off his left hand at the wrist. At least it had been his weaker hand.

Dinner came and went uneventfully. The bread was soggy, and the steaks went cold only minutes after Ted removed them from the pan.

Ted attempted to get a fire going again, but soon the evening was over and still no flame. They went to bed peacefully anyway, huddling together underneath the blankets.

Late in the night, Diane's mind rose from deep slumber. Something felt wrong. Her heart filled with a prescient terror. She tried to shake it and sleep on, but the fear wouldn't leave her alone.

The baby moved in her belly, kicking slightly as it shifted. It wriggled inside of her, almost shivering. Still half-asleep, Diane rubbed her stomach, trying to quiet the child, but the baby's restlessness continued unabated.

Diane woke fully and pushed the sheets and comforter on top of Ted. He mumbled lightly and turned over.

She slipped her feet off the four-poster bed and sat up. She waited for a moment, letting her baby's weight settle, before she stood up.

Diane walked slowly to the door. The rug underneath her feet felt sopping wet, but she couldn't hear any rain on the roof. Even the wooden floor felt mushy as she opened the bedroom door.

Fog covered the landing outside, and the banister gleamed with droplets of water. The landing felt soaked underfoot, just like the bedroom. Diane looked down into the living room and screamed.

At first, Diane thought a person stood in a puddle in front of the open front door. But glints of moonlight reflected off the creature's slimy hide. A tangled mess of weeds hung from the creature's head, and a greasy ichor dripped from claws on its hands and feet.

The creature turned to look at Diane. Dark grey orbs with red irises narrowed, and the creature screeched at Diane.

The sound paralyzed Diane, causing her vision to shimmer with nausea. The creature lurched toward the stairs, stealing every step it could toward her.

Diane turned her ashen face to watch Ted scramble out of the bedroom with a shotgun. Her gaze returned to the creature, and she heard him gasp as he spotted it, too.

Six blasts in rapid succession reverberated through the house. Diane watched Ted's body rock from the recoil of each shot. Smoke curled from the end of the semi-automatic shotgun, heat rising in waves off the barrel.

Two of the shots blew a gigantic, gooey hole in the creature, causing its torso to collapse on one side. The other four left jagged holes climbing the wall of the house.

Blobs of muck spattered the wall behind the intruder. It groaned, then collapsed in on itself. The scattered blobs started inching toward the mound of muck, then gathered speed. A few more seconds, and the attacker had reconstituted itself. It bellowed at Ted, then started up the stairs.

Ted shouted, "God damn! This thing must be one of them Kappa my grandfather always talked about! I thought he was just making his World War II stories more exciting!" He turned the shotgun over in his hands, holding it by the still-hot barrel, which adrenaline must have made cold.

Diane wanted to shout for him to stop — he would hurt his hands without harming the Kappa — but she could barely keep her knees from buckling. Ted let out a feral cry that contained fear as well as anger and attacked the Kappa with the butt of the shotgun.

Ted's blows rained down on the Kappa's head, and it backed down the stairs. Shouting wildly, Ted knocked the creature back, while Diane edged toward the bedroom door. Close to the middle of the living room, the stock on the shotgun broke into splinters. The expectant mother wanted to follow behind her husband and help fight the intruder off, but the life inside her made her retreat. "Ted! The axe! Get the axe!"

"Thanks, darling!" Ted pulled the axe off the wall, giving it a few practice swings. The Kappa hesitated a moment, then lurched towards the farmer again. Ted swung and missed, imbedding the sharp steel into the wall. The creature swiped a clawed hand across Ted's chest, leaving behind five red lines streaked with venomous ichor. Ted's arms and legs suddenly tightened in paralysis, and he fell.

Diane's heart lurched when Ted's face contorted in pain.

A growl erupted from deep in Ted's chest. "It's after the baby, Diane! Grandpa always said they fed on babies first! Keep it away from the baby!"

Lee Lackey

Diane's mind reasserted control over the terror in her body, and she ran back into the bedroom. The Kappa bellowed behind her, sloshing its way up each step.

Tears ran down Diane's face as she looked around the room. Ted kept only the shotgun in the bedroom, leaving the rest of his guns in a case downstairs. All the knives were in the kitchen, and her sewing scissors were in the living room.

Diane opened one of the windows and looked down to a two-story drop. She couldn't see anything she could use to climb down. The drop would probably injure her and kill the baby.

She turned to bar the door, but a wet chortle behind her told her she was too late. The creature stood in the middle of the room, a horrible grin on its face, rusty red teeth gleaming in the moonlight. It reached a claw out towards Diane's swollen stomach, and she felt her baby recoil inside her.

Diane's mind raced, trying to think of something, anything. Nothing fit — nothing could stop this horrible creature from eating her baby. Finally, a passage from the book on etiquette entered her mind, and she spoke before she had time to think.

"I'm terribly sorry, Mr...er...Kappa, we've been terrible hosts," Diane said nervously. She tried to calm herself and steel her emotions. She managed to smile.

The Kappa blinked a couple of times and its claws hovered hesitantly. The only sound was water dripping from the creature's legs to the puddle at its feet. It let out a throaty, gurgly, "What?"

Doing her best to make her smile look sincere, Diane said, "Well, we've been terrible hosts, after all. You've been a guest in our home for... all this time, and have been met by nothing but histrionics. I deeply apologize for our rudeness. You must let us fix something to eat for you!"

The muddy globs on the Kappa's face twitched, as something in the Kappa fought its way to the surface. After a few moments, the Kappa relaxed into an almost genteel stance. "Why, of course. It's been a long time since I've been a guest. I must apologize for my beastly behavior. Hunger has driven me mad for the past couple of decades. I shall fix the damage my presence has caused at a later time."

The Kappa looked longingly at Diane's belly, and wildness nearly resurfaced in his eyes. But Diane noticed the polite side resurface, and the Kappa left the bedroom.

The gentle hiss and pop of the pan filled the kitchen. The sulfurous odor of the propane stove burner couldn't drown out the meaty pork odor of the pan's contents. Diane attempted to stir the pan and then adjust the temperature control with the same hand, causing her to drop her tongs.

As she bent down to pick them up, the gentle murmur of her husband's whimpers filled the air. They were hard to bear, but she had to concentrate on her cooking if she didn't want to waste the meat in the pan. The Lord knew it had cost her dearly.

Beside her husband at the wooden table, the Kappa dripped steadily onto the rug below. It smacked its lips gently, like a cow anticipating cud.

The meat in the pan gently seared and browned into a delicate, lopsided star shape. Taking the pan from the fire, Diane set it on the table. She instinctively reached for the tongs with her left hand, only to pull back the home-bandaged stump when she remembered. Sighing, she used her right hand instead to lift its sister off the pan onto the Kappa's plate.

Ted's face was white; he looked everywhere but the kitchen table.

When he had heard of Diane's agreement, he'd argued and pleaded with her not to do it. He demanded she let him make the sacrifice. She had explained over and over: they couldn't let their child be lost, they needed all of Ted's strength to work the farm, and the Kappa promised rain for the parched fields.

But nothing had convinced him, her determination only frightening him all the more. Finally, she took the deed into her own hands, using the axe Ted had embedded into the wall during his fight with the Kappa.

Through the whole process, her husband had looked on the verge of attacking, whether her or the Kappa, she didn't know. The creature had watched with fascination and hunger, but had kept itself carefully reserved.

The hell of it was, her hand still hurt as if it remained attached. It was a sort of odd burning pain — a last stab at its destroyer — along with, of course, the throbbing agony of the wound itself. She had screamed, at first, but she had kept chopping until the hand was off and ready to cook.

A crunch of bone came to Diane's ears as she kept her gaze down, and a loud thump indicated Ted could not stand the sound of the Kappa eating a part of his wife.

On the periphery of her vision, the woman could see the measured movements of the Kappa as it relished every bite of its meal. Long, wet glomps and grunts were interspersed with slow gulps.

Lee Lackey

After several minutes, the creature began slowing down. It said, "I have not had such a meal in some time. You are a very generous host."

Diane rubbed a temple with her one hand, stifling a groan. "I'm glad... glad... glad you like it." She was trying very hard to keep up the charade of hospitality, but the sight of the beast eating its meal shook her to her core.

"Indeed, you are very strong, and the sacrifice you've made will ensure the rains for years to come. I haven't tasted this power since I left my homeland."

The pregnant woman set her head on the table, pushing down tears. She wanted to be somewhere — anywhere — but here, talking to the creature eating her hand. But the creature was civil, almost to the extreme, and she didn't know how it'd react to her sadness — offer to snack on her eyes, maybe.

Thankfully, the creature looked oblivious to her woes. "You've provided much nourishment today. Your child is truly blessed to have such a strong mother." A final snap of its jaws, and it had finished the entree. The creature rose. "I appreciate the hospitality, but I must return to my home. The air is much too dry for one such as me. Come and visit me anytime you wish. Our pact and bond is sealed so long as you live."

Moisture trailed behind the creature as it left. Even the normal night sounds remained silent until it left, and then the normal creaks of the house and sighs of the wind returned.

The light of morning turned the sky a rosy hue, but Diane's mood remained dark. She glared at her husband, who remained passed out on the floor, bitterly hating his cowardice. It wasn't his hand, and he couldn't even stay conscious. Then she thought of him sitting at the table, a piece of him being eaten by a monster, and

Lee Lackey

she wept at the thought. Perhaps he wasn't so weak, after all. In his place, she would've run screaming from the house.

As the sun rose, Diane managed to wake Ted so they could clean the horrid remains of her sacrifice. It took an amazingly short time to erase all signs of the amputation.

Ted stood silently beside Diane as she helped him do the dishes. Diane could tell he wanted to say something, but she wanted to let him work up the nerve to say it.

"Diane, how could you do that to yourself? And still be so polite? My nerves were jumping outta my head, and I could only think of killing it or running away," Ted said sheepishly.

Diane rubbed her swollen belly and said, "Hon, sometimes all it takes is a little civility."

Raindrops pitter-pattered on the tin roof overhead.

Look for Lee's first novel, exclusively from Grey Gecko Press, this fall.

Lee Lackey

Misty Mountain Morning

Leo King

The morning sun shone over the tall, smoky mountains of Abaline, the pale-gold sky littered with wispy, blanket-like clouds still parting from the heavy blanket of the previous night. The dew evaporated as the sun's rays chased away the nighttime cold, making a slowly rising mist that gave the grassy mountainside a dreamy quality.

Built into the forested slope of this sleepy mountain was a quaint and comfortable cottage, constructed of logs and topped with a heavy forest of thatch. From within the cottage, the scent of sweet maple wafted. A door, made of several lengths of birch cut and nailed together, served as the only entrance into this cozy abode.

As the door opened, young Bianca stepped out, dressed in a simple sky-blue colonial-style dress with a white apron, and greeted the day with a stretch and a yawn.

Still in her twelfth year, Bianca had yet to fully blossom. Her frame was slender and undeveloped, yet her face still had some of the roundness of childhood. Her tanned skin was still without the blemishes of adolescence, and her stature was still quite short. But being nearly thirteen years old, Bianca was starting to gain height, her face was becoming more mature, and her delicate dark locks were losing some of their childish curl.

"Bianca," called the matronly voice of her mother from inside the cottage, "is your brother with you?"

Bianca didn't reply, instead giving her arms and back another good stretch.

"Bianca," called out her mother's voice, this time with more force, "answer me, girl, or so help me, I'll come out there and box your ears!"

Letting out a sharp squeak, Bianca turned toward the dark interior of the cottage and called out, "Sorry, Mama! No, I haven't seen Ebby anywhere!"

The voice inside the cottage sounded annoyed. "He's probably playing on the other side of the mountain. Please go get him. Your father will be home for breakfast soon!"

Bianca gave a sigh underneath her breath; however, the smell of maple from within the cottage was more than a good enough motivator.

"All right, Mama," called Bianca as she reached into the large front pocket of her simple dress, where she usually kept several things secret to a young girl, such as the petals of particularly lovely flower, or scraps of string or ribbon she planned to sew into her clothes one day, and pulled out a plain bonnet. Securing it around her head, the girl started down the path leading to the other side of the mountain.

"Make sure your brother isn't eating any wild berries like last time," Bianca's mother called out as the girl headed away. "If he gets another stomachache, and we have to take him down to the valley to see Doctor Farrar, your father will be very upset."

"Okay," Bianca yelled, but she knew she was out of her mother's earshot. That fact didn't bother her; she felt that this morning was too nice to worry about errant younger brothers and their habit of putting anything in their mouths that they could get their hands on.

Following along the mountain trail, Bianca stepped around the boulders and bushes dotted the path.

When I get bigger, Bianca thought, *I'm going to go try and leap right over Lover's Gulch. They say that anyone who makes that jump on their first try will meet their true love the very next full moon.*

Bianca, whose thoughts had only recently started turning to boys, sighed inwardly at the thought of meeting her "prince."

Turning a sharp corner, Bianca suddenly found herself on the other side of the mountain, the bright rays of the morning sun hitting her square in the face. For a moment, Bianca was blinded, not just by the sun, but by its rays reflecting off the shiny metallic Tower of Life shimmering in the distance. The girl moved toward a shady spot to get out of the direct rays of the sun and then took a moment to look up at the distant monolith.

The Tower of Life stood like a deity, the massive structure seemingly reaching into the heavens, a silver shape amongst a range of tree-covered mountains. A tapered cylinder in shape, the Tower rose from the earth in a slant, its narrow end pointing in the direction of where the sun rises.

Like all of her people, Bianca had been raised on tales of the Tower of Life and how, many millennia ago, it came from the Heavens to the world of Abaline and produced the ancestors of her ancestors. Of the Twelve Tribes that rose from that miraculous creation, all but one left for other lands. Bianca's tribe, the Mountain

Tribe, stayed behind to live a simple life and, more importantly, to tend to the Tower of Life.

Like most in the Mountain Tribe, Bianca's family gave reverence each day to the Tower of Life. And like all members of the Mountain Tribe, Bianca would be required, on the day of her fourteenth birthday, to pilgrimage to the Tower of Life and be presented to the Grand Chieftain. That day still seemed so far off – the day she would be recognized as an adult.

Finally, the girl was snapped from her reverie by the scream of an eagle high above. Looking up and away from the Tower, Bianca watched the majestic bird fly high above, looking no larger than a speck of dust. Even with its tiny size, she could make out the impressive wingspan and hear its powerful cry, for all her people were gifted with spectacular vision.

Bianca smiled broadly, her mouth open as she cried back at the eagle with all the love of life in her heart, "Scree! Scree! Screeeee!"

The eagle circled around where Bianca was, as if watching the girl with amusement.

Continuing her journey, Bianca finally reached the slope of the mountain that led down past a gully, ending at the bank of a river where she and her brother usually played. The girl knew that if her little brother was anywhere, he would be there.

Bianca's mood seemed indomitably cheerful as she started skipping. She accompanied herself by first humming, then singing, a folk song passed on from her parents:

> *Every morning on the mountain*
> *We hold our hands and pray*
> *For the Tower, the lovely Tower*

Leo King

Shines on us, night and day
We are blessed, we are holy
Chosen ones, simple and clean
And we bathe in the Tower's glory
On this world of Abaline

As she finished singing, Bianca looked ahead and saw that she was at the gully, the halfway point between the start of the slope and the riverbank. Jumping over to the other side, the girl felt her stomach growl, and her cheerful thoughts suddenly turned to the breakfast she would undoubtedly be late for, and all because her little brother had gone off again.

"Ebby," Bianca growled to herself, "you better be in danger of getting eaten by a monster, or so help me, little brother, I'll swat your butt!"

With renewed vigor, and the thought of potentially swatting her brother's hiney, Bianca's skip broke into more of a jog. As she all but flew down the mountainside, she started singing again, this time singing a far more raucous song that she had once heard some boys sing:

Oh my Bessie has a bottom
It's about a mile wide
And when she goes a-dancing
Everybody hides
Each time there is a party
The world begins to quake
Because my dear sweet Bessie
Gives her butt a shake

Leo King

Bianca liked singing this song because the thought of anyone having a butt a mile wide was the funniest thing she had ever tried to imagine.

A few minutes later, Bianca reached the bottom of the mountain and was at the forested bank of the river. She took a few moments to catch her breath, and then she was fine and scouting about the riverbank for her little brother.

"Ebby," Bianca called out, looking about the tree-branches and the shore for any sign of her younger sibling, "Ebby, can you hear me? It's Bia!"

There was no reply, and Bianca was starting to get nervous. While it was likely that her little brother was poking around in something he shouldn't, there was always the chance he had gotten himself hurt. Even though the river wasn't very large, the current could still carry off a boy the size of her kid brother with ease. And so, making a cone with her hands, Bianca started to call out again.

"Ebby!" Her voice rang out over the riverbank. "Where are you? It's Bia! Please answer me, Ebby!"

Again no response. Even when he was horsing about, her little brother rarely did not respond.

"Ebby," Bianca called out a third time, her voice more frantic, "please, can you ans—"

"Over here, Sis," called out her brother's voice at long last. It came from a protective grove of trees near the river's shore.

Bianca breathed a sigh of relief, and vowed to box her little brother's ears when the moment presented itself. Moving along the shoreline of the river, Bianca pushed away the branches that got in her face, trying her best not to get her hair caught up in it. When she finally found her little brother, he was hunched over the area in the center of the trees by the shoreline, poking at something with a stick.

Her brother was like her, and everything from his tanned skin to his dark hair and dark eyes marked him as her brother. They even had similar faces, although Ebony's was still round with baby fat. He was dressed in a simple tunic and trousers.

"Ebony Easternling," Bianca yelled, hands disapprovingly on her hips, "what on earth are you doing?"

"Poking at some bugs," replied the eight-year-old boy with that sort of emphatic honesty that only an eight-year-old boy can possess.

Bianca felt an eyebrow twitch as she watched the small boy poke at what looked like a shiny gray egg. The egg was partially buried in the mud, one side was cracked open, and out of that crack swarmed what looked like dozens of little white bugs.

"Ugh," said Bianca, "what is that? Bugs crawling out of an egg? Ebby, don't play with that. For all you know, some poor bird's egg fell out of the nest and cracked open, and now those bugs are eating the poor, dead baby bird inside."

"That would be neat," Ebony replied.

"That would be disgusting," Bianca retorted.

The boy seemed more interested in his bug-poking than in his older sister, which only made her that much more annoyed. Leaning forward against one of the trees, the girl watched as her little brother poked the gray egg so hard it turned over, making more white bugs spill out. Shaking her head, Bianca asked, "Why you wanna be so mean to those poor bugs?"

"Because," Ebby replied, "I like to watch them run around."

Sighing, Bianca closed her eyes and began to lecture, as her mother once did when she was five years old and caught pulling the feathers off a bird. "Ebby, it's not nice to be mean to other living things. All creatures, great and small, are equal in the shadow of the Tower of Life. Don't you know that?"

Bianca opened her eyes just in time to see her little brother scoop up a handful of those scurrying bugs and put them in his mouth.

"Oh, gross," cried out Bianca, getting pale in the face and weak in the knees. "What the hell is wrong with you, Ebby? Ugh!"

"Crunchy," was all the boy said as he munched, dark bug juice dribbling out of the corners of his mouth. His teeth were filled with dark-colored bug guts.

Feeling nothing but revulsion for what her brother had done, Bianca jumped onto the gray egg and started stomping with her calloused soles. She could feel the egg crunching underneath her feet, as if it were filled with hundreds of tiny bones. When she was done with her holocaust, all the tiny white bugs were dead, and the egg was cracked in dozens of places.

"There," said the girl, catching her breath, "no more of those disgusting bugs for you to eat, you crazy child."

"You killed 'em all," Ebony said, his bottom lip pouting. "That's not fair! I wasn't done playing with them."

Bianca felt like arguing; however, feeling the futility of continuing the conversation, she got down to her little brother's level and tried to wipe the mud and bug juice off of his face, neck, arms, and hands. It was more of a mess than the girl could handle, however, so she instructed her little brother to go wash off in the river, ruffling his hair and saying that if he behaved, she wouldn't tell Mama and Papa about his bug-eating.

Ebony nodded and promised to be good, then scampered a few yards away to wash off. While her little brother rinsed the remaining mud and bug juice off of himself, Bianca sat down and started to scrape the mud and dead bugs off her feet.

As she scraped the bugs off, one of them moved. The sudden motion made the girl jump. With a quick swat, she squashed the bug against the sole of her foot.

Looking closely at her hand, with the acute vision gifted to her people, Bianca saw that the white bug had only four legs, and that the white skin seemed to be some kind of thick skin, dotted with unusual little bumps and knots, not the exoskeleton one would expect an insect to have. And its head was most odd — a circular shape with a single black rectangle for an eye.

"What kind of bug is this?" Bianca asked herself and reached down to pick up the flattened egg. It was large enough that she had to use both hands to pick it up.

Despite being severely cracked, the egg was remarkably intact, and weighed more than Bianca felt an egg should weigh. The surface also felt odd, more like holding a tin can than an egg, and as Bianca turned the egg around in her hands, she saw an unusual design on the side. It looked like a rectangle made of red and white stripes, with a corner of that rectangle a dark blue, decorated with many little white dots.

"Huh. I've never seen an egg like this before," Bianca said to herself. For a moment, she thought about putting it in the pocket of her apron and bringing it home for Papa to see, but then she thought better of it.

I'm supposed to be learning the lessons of my Ancestors, Bianca thought, *to respect all of life, as all life is precious before the Tower of Life. If Papa and Mama knew I killed a bunch of stupid bugs, I'd never hear the end of it.*

With that thought, Bianca tossed the egg into the river, where it promptly sank. The girl then spent a few minutes washing herself clean of the mud of dead bugs.

When she was done, she looked for Ebony, who was at the start of the path back up the mountain, jumping on some rocks. Sighing inwardly again at the role of being a big sister, Bianca collected her little brother and, taking hold of his hand, led him up the mountain trail and back home.

In the distance, the Tower of Life shone in the sun over the peaceful forested mountain range. The flora all across the range looked to be covered in the cobwebs of smoky haze, the morning dew having long since evaporated.

It was a beautiful misty mountain morning.

The Faithful Farmers

B.H. Werner

"It's no good," declared Rizzerab solemnly, holding open one of the two bags of food our tribe had left. Hot wind threw stinging sand at his exposed calves and flapped his tattered clothes like white flags waving.

Though the scores of my fellow tribesmen might have missed it, I could see that sadness had begun collecting in the newly developing creases at the corners of his eyes. There was a moment of silence as we all absorbed the news, and new trickles of despair filled the dark cracks in our minds, nourishing our long-unspoken fears.

"Impossible!" yelled young, fiery Grattic, his voice like a hammer shattering the delicate moment. "That stuff doesn't go bad unless it rots from moisture. Do you see any moisture around here? NO! We haven't seen as much as a puddle in three days. That's why we brought it!"

"You can see for yourself if you like," Rizzerab returned calmly, holding the bag out for anyone to see.

Grattic stomped up to him, sand flying from his sandals. Grabbing the bag away from Rizzerab, Grattic peered inside. But there was no encouragement to be found in the loosely woven wool sack. His face began to contort, twitching back and forth between anger and mounting fear.

"We can pick out the rotten bits. Eat the rest. There's no need to throw out the whole thing," Grattic said, half-ordering, half-begging.

"You know as well as I do that if one piece is tainted, the whole bag is tainted," Rizzerab said, reminding us of a lesson we'd all known since we were tall enough to pick the fields and cure meat. "You can eat it, but you'll just go mad before you die."

Grattic backed away in defeat, his tattered shoes dragging.

Several miles off, a bandit tracker held crumbling bits of sandal leather in his hand. He'd almost lost the fleeing farmers a few times since they left their village, the wind-blown sand covering their tracks, but as soon as their sandals began to succumb to the desert, tracking them became much easier.

"How close are we?" asked a giant, sinewy bandit wearing a linen vest and a helmet bearing a ram's horns.

"A few days at this pace, maybe less," replied the tracker, his voice slick as a wet snake.

"Good," said the giant bandit stoically. "Prophecy or no, we must kill them all. Carry their heads back on pikes and set them about the main roads."

"I share your thirst, Highest Annonto, but if I may ask, why go to all this trouble? We already have their stores. They've got little on them of any worth now."

Annonto shifted his gaze to the tracker, who lowered his shoulders in deference, worried he'd offended his leader.

But Annonto replied, "We must make an example of them. If we let them go, it may embolden others to defy us. And if we simply let them expire quietly in the desert, people may tell stories that they escaped us. Their quiet deaths could turn to legend and undo us."

The tracker nodded his head in understanding. This wasn't about one tribe of rebellious farmers. This was about ensuring every tribe they raided on their circuit stayed docile and handed over provisions.

This was about keeping the tribes under control, even when they had to raid two, three, four times a year to accommodate their swelling numbers. This was about the bandits' entire way of life.

That night Rizzerab sat near me as we gathered around the fire. We all tried to make our thumb-sized rations stretch as far as we could, nibbling at them with little to break the silence but the crackling of the fire and the occasional hushed secret.

I worried that the ever-blowing wind might carry their doubting whispers up to the spirits. Then again, if we were fulfilling a prophecy, as the elders seemed to think, there'd be little we could do to alter our path.

Rizzerab turned toward me to say something; the words caught in his chest before they came out.

"Why does Grattic doubt the gods so strongly?" Rizzerab whispered, almost as if the very words would offend them.

"The old have much faith to fall back on. They have whole lifetimes of it stored up," I said. "What is it to them if their lives are cut a few years short? Easier to believe for just a bit longer and die believing than to question everything that's made them."

"But what does that have to do with Grattic?" Rizzerab asked.

B.H. Werner

"The young have less faith to fall back on," I explained. "Our faith has done less for us than it has for the old. We remember yearly bandit raids on our village when we were young, and now we know gods that seem determined to kill us before our time. Would you want to believe in gods that let bandits steal your food and lead you into the desert to have your bones picked clean by buzzards?"

"I see," said Rizzerab, his deep voice full of understanding, his sharp features like stone in the flickering firelight. "Where does that leave me?"

"Somewhere in between," I said. "You probably have the best perspective of all."

"Or the worst," he mumbled.

"What?" I asked, wondering if he'd repeat it.

"Nothing," he said quietly and turned back to the fire.

That night, I recited the prophecy as I drifted off to sleep, as the elders had instructed us all to do, as if thinking it would make it so. I tried to ignore the beastly growl of Immin's stomach next to me as I retraced the verses.

If your trials become too great, take up and
flee the land of your fathers.

Your feet will ache from wandering, but lose
not your faith.

For the message of your delivery will come
from a spirit of the sky.

It will lead you to the end of your wandering,
and great hunger will be satisfied,
beginning a new era.

B.H. Werner

The next day, Degas and Hermis wore their worry on their faces. Up until now, they had taken the journey the easiest of any of us. Degas was an exiled warrior from across the sea.

Hermis was a hunter from another tribe to the west that came to us when he took on one of our women, Irien, as a bride. I wondered if Degas and Hermis sensed the bandits getting closer. If anyone knew, they would.

At midday, when we stopped to rest, all our worries began to bubble up.

"We must make a stand," demanded Josot, a peevish, weak-armed man whose wife was tending to their crying children.

"We cannot fight them," replied Rizzerab, always the voice of reason.

"They'll catch up to us any day now. Better to stop now and fight rested than to be chased down exhausted on the dunes!"

"With what would you fight them?" Rizzerab asked wearily, his voice full of the exasperation of a parent questioning a child who declares his intent to jump off a tall rock.

"Degas and Hermis for starters," Josot retorted, waving his gangly arms demonstratively. "They know their way around a spear."

All eyes turned to the two men, except Immin, whom I noticed eying one of our number like a plains cat eyes a sick doe. The target's name was Orin, and he was the fattest of us.

Not to say that he was fat any longer. He had just started the journey with more to lose about the waist than the rest of us, leaving him the meatiest of us now.

B.H. Werner

"They are only two," said Rizzerab. "Two cannot stand against an entire army."

"We'll take up our implements!" Josot exclaimed, full of the fire of a man who'd never been to war. His wife was having no luck calming his children.

"Taking up a weapon doesn't make you a soldier," shot back Rizzerab, beginning to lose his patience for the first time I'd ever seen. "If you arm your waddling son, does that make him a warrior? Or does it take more than arms and a thresher?"

In the pause between them, I thought I heard the clinking of metal over a nearby dune. Degas must have heard it, too, because his gaze swung from Josot to the dune as well.

Josot was red in the face now, screaming so the whole desert could hear. "We must do something, but what do you care, Rizzerab? You have no sons to be killed. You have no wife or daughters to be raped!"

Rizzerab's face flashed to anger, and he loosed the dagger in his belt. His wife's death years ago had been brutal, and the reasons he was childless were very sore for him.

"All children are the children of the tribe!" Rizzerab yelled. "And all wives are the responsibility of the tribe! Now stop flapping your tongue before I take it from you," he threatened, knuckles white as he gripped his dagger.

Seeing Rizzerab's rage, Josot slinked back, retreating under the guise of tending to his children. In the silence, I heard a clink again. This time, it caught Hermis's attention, too.

I looked at both of them and back up at the ridge of the dune. They looked at each other with instant understanding and bolted in all-out sprints toward the noise, spears in hand.

When they returned a short bit later, they dragged a bloody bandit with them, spear wounds dotting his lifeless body.

"A scout," Hermis pronounced.

"Wonderful!" Josot said, hope returning to his face. "Now they'll never find us. Fantastic!"

"Wrong," said Degas. "They wouldn't send out just one scout. They'd send out several in specific directions. When this one doesn't return, they'll know which direction we went."

Josot's eyes went wide. "Then why'd you kill him?!"

"Because if we hadn't, they would have found out which direction we're going even sooner," Degas replied flatly.

Josot collapsed into sobs on the ground.

Degas scowled at Josot's dramatics. Hermis just sighed.

"I hope this prophecy finds us soon," I said softly to Rizzerab.

"I, too," he replied.

As evening fell, Annonto looked upon three of the four scouts he'd send out. Turning to his men, he thrust a finger in the direction of the scout that hadn't returned. They marched.

The following day, Orin didn't turn up for rations. We gathered and accounted for everyone else, but he was not among us.

B.H. Werner

We sent people to search nearby, thinking perhaps he'd run off too far in order to relieve himself, but he was nowhere to be found.

Hermis found no tracks leading away from us, but wasn't sure he would find them today anyway, owing to the high wind.

Immin, however, looked unusually satisfied. I casually crept closer to him. His famously loud stomach wasn't growling. Not so much as a gurgle.

No, I thought, *it couldn't be*, remembering the way Immin had been eying Orin. I wandered around, half searching, half trying to decide whether I was going to tell anyone about my suspicions.

Finally, feet aching, I plopped down in the sand. *I'm probably just trying too hard to put pieces together that aren't there,* I thought. I peered out at the dunes, trying to regain what little was left of my sanity before I made dangerous accusations.

Satisfied I'd regained some of my composure, I hoisted myself up and headed back toward the place where we'd decided to take our day's rest. On the way down the final dune, my foot caught on something hard and I went tumbling down the sand.

Angry that I'd been so wrapped up in my thoughts that I'd gone rolling down the hill before the gods and everybody, I ran back up to curse the rock I'd stubbed my toes on. But something about it was strange.

It was different than any of the rocks I'd seen in weeks. It appeared to have flesh clinging to it, too. I tugged at it, realizing it was wedged in the sand pretty well. I dug around it, throwing hot sand behind me like a dog digging for a bone.

Except that it was a bone. I kept digging and found more of them. A human skeleton, strips of half-wet flesh still dangling from it. I hollered for the others.

Immin had eaten Orin. I hadn't wanted to believe it, but I trusted my eyes more than I trusted that greedy simpleton.

"You think I did what?" Immin screamed, squirming on the ground with Rizzerab, Degas and I on top of him, Degas's knife to his throat.

"Then where is he?" asked Rizzerab.

"He took off last night. Said he thought he had a better chance on his own," whimpered Immin.

"Why are you just telling us about this now?" demanded Degas. Immin gulped, releasing a small drop of blood where his throat touched the knife.

"He gave me his ration for the day to keep my mouth shut."

"Why would he do that?"

"I don't know, maybe he thought you'd try to stop him."

"And the skeleton?"

"I have no idea," Immin said, eyes begging to be let go. "Maybe someone else died in the forsaken land. It *is* a desert. And there *are* bandits. We buried one of their scouts the same way just yesterday!"

He had a point, but the evidence was too strong to completely dismiss it.

"Do you really think I could eat a whole man myself?" Immin asked indignantly.

B.H. Werner

"Perhaps you didn't work alone," said Degas. "Perhaps you had accomplices who are better at hiding their satisfaction."

In the end, we weren't certain Immin had made a meal of Orin, but we couldn't take the risk. We bound Immin's arms and dragged him along as we headed onward, worried we'd already wasted too much time with the bandits almost certainly gaining on us more quickly than we wanted to admit.

Miles away, Orin stood in front of Annonto, spitting out the tribe's whereabouts between flying crumbs of eagerly eaten bread.

The next day, almost nobody spoke. We needed to travel fast. Our lives depended on it. Hermis had caught glimpses of dust kicked up by the bandits less than a mile away several times. Parents carried children if they had to. The elderly were tossed upon carts or helped on by younger relatives. Rizzerab lead the way.

Our chances seemed slim. The wind wasn't blowing to cover up our tracks today. Without a miracle, we'd all be hacked into buzzard food before sundown. I cursed the gods. What good were they? What had they done for us? If they were real, I imagined them watching us with great entertainment, greedily absorbing our praises and placing wagers on how long we'd last.

"Why do you curse those who would save you?" asked a strange voice. It was high pitched, and sounded like many voices at once. I saw that the entire tribe had stopped to gaze at something hovering before them.

It was about two feet tall, and it had white skin, nose-less nostrils, four arms, and a long tail instead of legs. Its pupil-less silver eyes surveyed us, while its long, thin dragonfly wings buzzed softly. A purplish glow emanated from it; it was the color of Anshreki, the god of growth and healing. When it was confident it had the attention of every last man, woman and child, it spoke.

"I know what pursues you," it said. Several gasped. A few jaws dropped.

"And I know what you seek," it continued. The elders bowed on their swollen knees in the hot sand.

I couldn't believe the gods had actually sent the messenger the prophecy had promised.

"Follow me if you want to end your struggle. Follow me if you want to end your wandering. Follow me if you want to escape the horrors that have chased you across the desert."

The prophecy was coming true. I could hardly believe it, but the messenger was hovering right in front of us. Even the least faithful of us grabbed their packs with new vigor and began following the sky spirit.

It led us in a snaking pattern, staying low between the dunes so as not to alert the bandits to our exact whereabouts. Occasionally, the winged spirit would sweep its hand horizontally, and our tracks would disappear behind us.

I wasn't sure if it was from new hope or if the sky spirit helped quicken our steps, but we fled with divine speed.

As the sun dipped down to kiss the horizon, the dunes gave way to a huge, rocky hill. The sky spirit came to a stop and faced us. It pointed to the mouth of a cave, just taller than a man and just as wide.

B.H. Werner

"In there, your pursuers will not find you. Stay until I return, and you will never again have to worry about thirst, famine or murderous pursuers."

As we filed into the cavern and set down our things to rest, some wept with joy. Some lay down peacefully to nap. Some said prayers of thanks and burned incense in gratitude. We were finally safe.

All we had to do was wait here for a while until the bandits passed, and the sky spirit would lead us to a new land of safety and plenty. Overcome with relief, I myself started nodding off, until I heard screaming. Several of us ran to see what was wrong.

A small girl held up her hand, sobbing, a deep, sizzling burn in her palm.

"Some sort of green goo fell on her hand," the girl's mother said frantically."It was thick as jam. I wiped it off with a scrap of linen as quickly as I could, but it burned her so fast." The cloth sat smoldering on the cave floor.

"Everyone," Rizzerab's voice boomed, reverberating through the cave, and surprising many, "keep your eyes keen on the ceiling. There may be something dangerous falling. Don't let it touch you or..." But Rizzerab only got halfway through his warning before we heard a yell. A woman was trying to get her husband's sizzling shirt off. I heard a drip next to my foot and backed away. What was going on?

Josot made a dash for the mouth of the cave, leaving his wife and children behind, but the opening contorted, shifted and closed before he could get out, leaving us with only the light of our torches and lanterns.

Before we knew it, the goo was coming down like rain. Children hid beneath their parents. Parents hid under blankets. People hid under carts. Everyone hid under anything they could, but it didn't matter. The acid ate right through wood, metal, and cloth. Nowhere was safe.

I wished for absentee gods. I wished for gods that didn't care, because the ones we knew were going to make us suffer before they ended us. I felt the ground below me shift and toss me onto my side, exposing my other side to the acid rain. Then, torches flickered and went out as the entire cave shook and came alive.

Pain surged through me as the bones in my left arm were crushed by falling rocks. Drips of melting agony rained down on me. Stars pierced the blackness when a wagon wheel was thrown against my skull. I tried to brush the goo off my body with my good hand, even as I heard my right leg snap between shifting rocks. But it was useless. I barely had enough muscle left on my hands to make them work.

I heard some beg the gods for mercy, but I didn't. I knew no mercy was coming. The sounds of crunching and abruptly ended screams tormented my ears. The sizzling smoke from all the wounds choked my lungs with a putrid gas. I could tell they were filling with blood. I gasped for air, wishing that the afterlife would come quickly. It couldn't be worse than this.

As I was about to lose consciousness from the pain, I realized that this wasn't a cave. It was a stomach. It tightened and undulated, crushing and digesting us, until surely nothing would be left but our empty farming village so many miles away.

Outside, a woman covered in tattoos of runes and symbols long forgotten patted the hill like a mother burping a baby. She leaned in close to the stone and

B.H. Werner

whispered dotingly, "One more meal like that, and you'll be ready to hatch."

She withdrew a soft hand from the rocks and turned to her partner, Aezle, who was hovering a few feet above the ground, her dragonfly wings a blur. "How did you get them here so quickly?"

"You only need to know what someone is looking for," said Aezle. "Become it, or promise it, and they'll do whatever you desire. These people were looking for a sky spirit to lead them to safety. So that's what I gave them."

The woman smiled. It was good to have such a crafty partner. "Think you can do it twice in one day?"

Aezle huffed indignantly and flew off into the night to find the bandits.

B.H. Werner

Hybrid

Austin Malone

Jacqueline tries to ignore the revving of engines out-side as she watches the wallscreen. The newscaster is a cartoon mouse, and that is her first clue that she is dreaming.

"We have breaking news," he squeaks. "The new line of BioGreen hybrid vehicles has discovered the ultimate fuel source. Some of our viewers have already witnessed the current eco-friendly trend, and we invite all of you at home to celebrate with us the erasure of humankind's carbon footprint. Do it quickly, though, because they're coming for you, Jax. And they are hungry."

An electric surge of adrenaline accelerates her heart rate, and she leans closer to the screen.

"This just in," the mouse says, pressing a paw to one oversized floppy ear. "We have just received word that Jacqueline Marx's life expectancy has been shortened to approximately ten seconds. Beginning now. In other news, pop-cap distribution centers will no longer be ac-cepting tuna warbles as payment."

The rest of the newscast is lost in the sudden implo-sion of her front window. She gasps and whirls around in time to see the bed of a pickup truck retreating from her living room. The snarl of engines grows louder, and a cherry-red compact car propels itself through the hole in her wall and angles toward her. The spikes of its harvest-

er-grille flash as they begin to spin in hungry anticipation.

She turns to run, and she knows that she won't make it. The air in her living room becomes viscous, slowing her flight, but not impeding the advance of the car. It takes her in midstride, her left foot snagged in the car's grille. With a jolt, she is wrenched from her feet, and she hits the floor facedown.

She hears a voice beside her urging her to her feet. "Jax! Get up!"

Jacqueline wants to get up, but she's seen what happens once a car brings someone down, and she knows she's done for. She tries to scream, but her vocal cords produce only a thin unsteady mewling which does nothing to block out the wet popping-tearing sound of her leg being drawn into the vehicle's mechanical maw.

How long now before it severs her femoral artery? She wonders how much of her the car will consume before she bleeds to death, and as her strength ebbs, she lowers her tear-streaked face to the carpet and closes her eyes. At least there's no pain. She'll be dead before the shock wears off.

The voice, harsh and masculine, comes again. This time, it is accompanied by a hand on her shoulder which gives her a rough shake.

"Jax. Wake the fuck up. We got incoming."

Jacqueline came to with a gasp, jackknifing upright in her bunk and slamming her head against the low concrete ceiling.

Dark eyes peered at her with concern from a beard-shadowed face, and her second-in-command, Remy, winced sympathetically as she clutched her head and let out a venomous stream of profanity.

"Sorry about that," he said, the crease in his brow visible even in the dim light. "But we need you topside."

"Yeah, yeah," she growled, swinging her feet — *both feet. Intact. Dear God, what a nightmare* — over the edge of the cot. "You said incoming. Cars?"

Remy shuddered. "No. One of Wesson's boys. Got a message he seems to think you'll want to hear."

"All right," she said, shrugging into her tac vest, then reaching for her rifle. "Let's go find out what Wesson wants."

The messenger was young and was as fair and clean-cut as Remy was dark and hirsute. He didn't hesitate to accept the share of rations that Jacqueline offered, and she and Remy waited patiently for him to eat before they questioned him.

"So," Jacqueline said, as the boy washed down his last mouthful of beans with a gulp from a bottle of water, "what's so important that Wesson couldn't wait until next month's trading session?"

The boy reached into his inner coat pocket and withdrew a small black box. "A strange thing happened a couple of days ago," he said, turning the box in his hands as he spoke. "Our phone rang."

Remy shook his head. "How is that possible?"

The boy grinned. "I know, right? For the first few rings, we just sat there staring at the phone like it was something from another planet. Wesson was the one who finally grabbed it, and after he realized who was on the other end, we figured making our phone ring wasn't such a big deal after all."

Austin Malone

"And who was on the other end?" Jacqueline supplied.

The boy's grin widened, and he set the box — a digital voice recorder — on the table. "Bachmann."

"Bullshit," Remy and Jacqueline exclaimed in unison.

"Heh," the boy chuckled. "That's the same thing Wesson said. Want to hear the conversation after that point?"

An hour later, after replaying the file several times, Jacqueline came to a decision. Remy regarded her with an even stare, his grey eyes peering at her from above steepled fingers. He would oppose her, she knew, no matter what she said. His constant dissent could be annoying at times, but more often than not, she valued his insights, finding that his counterpoints helped her to examine decisions in a more critical light.

As a schoolteacher in her former life, she had made a point of stressing the importance of critical thinking, and when Remy had first encountered her with her band of survivors — mostly made up of students whose addresses she had culled from the high school roster — he had been even more abrasive and contrary than he was now.

She welcomed him from the start, though, and had been delighted to learn about his military background. Despite the occasional angry mutterings then (and now) from her companions, there wasn't a single one of them who could deny Remy's hand in forging the community in which they lived today.

Austin Malone

Remy laced his fingers together, revealing a faint smile, and rested his chin upon his knuckles. "So how's it gonna be?"

"I say we go for it."

"We don't even know that it's really him, Jax."

"It doesn't matter," she replied. "Whether it's Bachmann or not, we have a lone survivor who wants to help fight the machines. In that respect, how is he different from any one of us? Furthermore, he managed to get a signal out to an actual phone. Think of what that could mean for the other groups all around the world."

Remy shrugged. "And what if it *is* Bachmann? We're talking about the guy who kickstarted this whole mess. There are plenty of folks here who would be more than willing to let him hang by his own noose. I mean, up 'til now we've all just assumed that he'd been eaten by one of his creations, and there's not one of us who didn't think of it as a sort of poetic justice."

"He's still trying, Remy," she said, softening her voice. "If it were you, wouldn't you like to be allowed the chance to fix the mess you created?"

The messenger boy, whose name was Josh, had been dozing on a bench; he woke with a start when Remy slammed his fist down on the aluminum table. "He's had a chance! Two, in fact, and he blew both of them."

"That's debatable," Jacqueline said. "When he uploaded the virus that took out the cars' central neural network, he ruined their ability to organize."

"Spoken like a true civilian," Remy grunted. "Trust me, Jax, a coordinated enemy is easier to handle than several million random aggressors."

Jacqueline shrugged. "Maybe, maybe not. But you know as well as I do that our group stands more of a chance against a single feral car than it does against a whole pack of them."

"Yeah? Well, what about that stunt he pulled when he hijacked the Star Wars systems?"

"Are you kidding? He demolished their ability to track over distance when he wiped out the satellites. If he had left the G.P.S. intact, they'd know the location of every band of survivors all over the world, and central neuronet or not, we'd have cars on our doorstep twenty-four-seven!"

Remy rolled his eyes. "Sure. You're right. It's way better being thrown back to the Dark Ages, and having to rely on human carrier pigeons for information."

Josh raised his hand. "Uh. I think I resent that."

Jax and Remy glared at him for a beat, and then they started laughing. Bewildered, Josh glanced from one to the other, waiting for them to wind down before speaking. "So, what's the plan, exactly?"

"Right," Jacqueline said. "We'll keep the operation tight. Just you and me, Remy."

"And me," Josh objected.

Remy snorted. "Not a chance, kid."

The boy blushed, but he didn't back down. "Sorry to bust your bubble, soldier, but I've got my marching orders, too. Wesson sent me here because this is the closest encampment to Bachmann's location. He gave you first dibs, but that doesn't mean you get to call all the shots.

"There's more at stake here than your little rat-hole commune. When I left, Wesson was organizing his own delegation, and they're probably on the way right now. If he gets here and finds out that you left me behind, he might take matters into his own hands."

Jacqueline chewed her lip, thinking, then nodded. "Fine. But we're not dragging dead weight. You keep up and stay sharp, or you're roadkill. Got it?"

"You betcha."

As Jacqueline stood to examine a map that was tacked to the wall behind her, Remy looked at Josh and frowned. "What exactly does Wesson want you tagging along for?"

Josh scooped up the voice recorder and waggled it under Remy's nose. "Documentation. Dunno if you noticed, but our boy Bachmann was kinda vague about his latest brainfart. Wesson trusts you two enough to take Bachmann in, but not so much to make a judgment on Dr. Fruitloop's most recent plan."

Remy grimaced. "Nice to know what Wesson really thinks of us."

"Hush," Jax said, motioning the two men over. "Come see. Remy, do you know the exact location of the amusement park in Springfield?"

Without a word, Remy snagged the red marker that hung on a string next to the map and slashed a quick "X" across one of the squares on the map's grid.

"Shit," Josh proclaimed as he looked at the spot. "That's across the river."

"No worries," Jacqueline said as she moved on to another map. "We've got a raft, and we've got tunnels that'll take us nearly all the way to the river."

She pulled a small notebook from her vest, and she wrote while she studied the second map. When she was done, she called Remy over and handed him the notebook. He glanced back and forth between the notebook and the map for several minutes and then nodded. "It's good. Take us about a day."

Austin Malone

"That's what I figured." Jax tapped the first map with her finger. "You used to live in Springfield. How long do you think it'll take us to get to Bachmann once we're across the river?"

Remy drummed his fingers on the table. "If we can leave within the next few hours, we'll hit the drainage canal by sunrise of day-after-tomorrow. From there, figure an hour to get to the river and prep the raft. If the weather's nice, we can make it across the river in about two hours. Then, it's just a couple of miles to the park. As long as we don't run into any trouble, we could have Bachmann back to the tunnels by that evening."

"Let's do it," Jax said, smiling. "Race you to the storeroom."

As Remy dashed from the room, Jacqueline was on her way out as well when she noticed that Josh hadn't budged. She clapped her hands and he twitched, his dazed expression sharpening as he focused on her.

"Let's go, kid," she barked. "This is it. If you're coming, then you'd better light a fire under your ass and get moving!"

Josh jerked to his feet and scrambled after her, stuffing the recorder back into his coat pocket. They jogged down the barely-lit twisting concrete corridors, and after their third turn down an unmarked tunnel, she realized that the boy was falling behind. He must have realized it as well.

With a grunt, he lengthened his stride; then he almost collided with her when she stopped in front of an opening on their right. She put out an arm to brace herself and rolled her eyes at Remy's arched eyebrow. His lips quirked, and he turned back to the paperwork he had been filling out.

Austin Malone

His pencil made a few more quick scratches, and then he handed the clipboard to a worried-looking young girl who twisted a strand of her thin blond hair around a finger while reading the requisition form. A second later, the girl's haunted eyes darted up, and fear flashed in them when she saw Josh peering over Jacqueline's shoulder.

"Ms. Marx?" Her voice was little more than a tremulous whisper.

Jax sighed. "Sandra, sweetheart, we've been over this before. Please call me Jacqueline. The Carmageddon leveled the field. You survived. That makes us equals."

"But..." Sandra tapped the clipboard with an unsteady finger. "This list. You're leaving? And who's that?" She swung the finger up to bear on Josh.

Jax stepped forward and reached out to clasp the outstretched hand. "Look at me, Sandra."

The girl's pale eyes flicked wide, then settled on an area around the tip of Jacqueline's nose.

Jax smiled. "You have to trust me, sweetheart. Remy and I are going out for a couple of days to follow a lead. I don't want to get your hopes up, but we might have hit on a solution to our car troubles. I don't have time to explain, but you'll want to talk to somebody, so go find Martha. Tell her we'll need bunks for..."

She trailed off and looked back at Josh. "Wesson still have that weird thing about the number five?"

Josh snorted. "Yup."

Jax nibbled at her lower lip for a moment as she thought it out. "So that's Wesson's crew, plus you, and one for our other guest. Seven bunks, then. Okay?"

Sandra nodded. A faint blush tinted her cheeks now, and the fear in her eyes was diluted by the excitement.

Austin Malone

Remy cleared his throat. "Tick tock, Sandra."

The girl jumped and snatched her hands free of Jacqueline's. "Right. Right away. Sorry."

As Sandra grabbed the clipboard, and scuttled off into the passageway behind her, Jax turned to face Remy.

"Asshole," she muttered.

Remy shrugged. "We don't have time for her poor-me act."

Jax took a quick step and restrained herself from kicking Remy in the shin. "That girl lost her entire family, you insensitive dick."

Remy pushed off the wall that he was leaning against and bent to glower into Jacqueline's face.

"We've all lost people we care about," he growled. "She needs to recognize that fact and get over it, and the way you coddle her isn't doing her any favors."

Jax opened her mouth to respond, but shut it as Sandra reappeared with a shopping cart full of gear. The girl took one quick look at Remy and Jax, then ducked her head and began to remove the equipment. At their feet, she placed three knapsacks and three elongated cylinders with straps attached to them.

As Jax and the two men strapped on the bags and the tubes, Sandra spoke, listing the contents. "Rations are in the main compartment of each pack, and flash-lights are in the front section along with the concussion grenades."

Josh rapped on his tube with his knuckles. "What's in here?"

"Spike strips," Remy said. "If we're attacked, lay down the spike strip and back off. You'll have about thirty seconds to toss a grenade under the car while it repairs its wheels. That'll knock out the sensory apparatus."

"Then what?" Josh said.

Jax chuckled. "Then you run like hell." Giving the girl a quick hug, she said, "Thanks, Sandra, and remember to talk to Martha about getting those bunks set up. Wesson and his crew will probably arrive by tomorrow evening."

Sandra nodded and whispered, "Good luck," as Jacqueline turned to follow Remy and Josh down the corridors.

They made a large portion of the trek in through the tunnels without speaking to one another. At first, the group made attempts to strike up conversation through devices like Twenty Questions or Six Degrees of Kevin Bacon. After a few hours, though, the drab surroundings leached all enthusiasm for such games, and they plodded on in silence.

After what seemed like days, the shaft began to lighten. At first, Josh thought he was hallucinating. His nerves were shot from the hours of sensory deprivation, and he was pretty sure that he had lost consciousness a couple of times, while his body continued to march zombielike after the others.

He rubbed his eyes and blinked and then squinted. "Is it...? I mean, are we...?"

Jax looked over her shoulder and smiled at him. "Yep. We're two turns away from the canal. We'll stop there for some grub, and then the easy part is over."

Sure enough, within a few minutes, they were seated on a long steel bench, eating Vienna sausages and fruit cocktail in the weak sunlight that filtered through

Austin Malone

the grid of the outlet's grate. Josh savored the opportunity to sit, and he tried to prolong the experience by eating at a slower rate than the others, but his empty stomach got the better of him. The scant repast was gone before he knew it, and his forlorn gaze drifted from his own empty tins to those of his companions.

Remy clapped him on the back. "Sorry, kiddo. No rest for the wicked. Now levitate your ass so I can get this locker open."

Josh stood and turned, realizing as Remy bent and fiddled with a couple of rusty clasps that the bench was in fact an oversized foot-locker. The lid swung open under Remy's guidance with a squeal of protest, and he leaned in and retrieved the contents. As Jax took the tubes of blue and yellow plastic from Remy's hands and began to assemble them, Josh breathed a sigh of comprehension.

"Aha. Paddles."

Jax winked. "Gold star for you, junior. Move to the head of the class."

Josh rolled his eyes. "So where's the boat?"

Remy slammed the lid of the locker with a bang. "In the river, genius. Do you actually want to see it, or would you rather sit here and ask stupid questions?"

"Asshole," Josh muttered, and Jax chuckled.

Remy ignored them both, snaking an arm through the grate to open it. Turning to Josh and Jax, he swept his other hand in a grand gesture toward the opening. "Ladies first."

Josh fumed, but he kept quiet as he followed Jax out onto the steep concrete slope of the canal. Remy joined them a moment later, letting the grate fall closed with a clang behind them, and pointed to a sheer cliff of concrete and steel girding about a half mile away on their right. "That's the spillway mechanism. Our raft is tethered up there."

Jax snorted and thrust an oar into Remy's gut. He grunted and took the oar, and she sneered as she deepened her voice and said, "Do you actually want to see the boat, or would you rather stand here and make stupid observations?"

Remy growled and took a swipe at her with the paddle, which she parried with her own. Then, giggling, she brought the flat end up to smack against his shin and dashed off toward the spillway. Cursing, Remy hobbled after her, as did Josh, albeit at a slower pace.

They made it to the raft and across the river without incident. After disembarking, they kept the steel frame of the amusement park's roller coaster in sight, and made their way at a steady pace through the detritus of the former civilization toward their rendezvous.

When the attack came, they were unprepared. Lulled by the silence of their surroundings, and so near to their goal, they had allowed complacency to replace vigilance. Deep in speculation about Bachmann's undisclosed plan, they skirted the ruins of an apartment complex which obscured the block ahead and detoured down an alley which led to a parallel street to their left.

As they emerged and once more oriented themselves toward the amusement park, they found themselves face-to-grille with a battered white pickup truck.

"Oh, God," whispered Jax. "Remy?"

"Fire escape," he said out of the corner of his mouth. "Halfway down the alley behind us."

Austin Malone

The truck's engine revved, a threatening snarl, and the blades in its grille whickered as they began to spin.

Remy popped the top of his tube and shook the spike strip out onto the ground at his feet. "Go. Now!"

Jax pivoted and dashed back to the mouth of the alley. She chanced a glance over her shoulder as she turned the corner. Remy was on her heels, but the boy was still standing, rooted to the spot they had just left.

Abandoning caution, she started back, shouting, "Josh!"

Remy caught her by the elbow and shook his head, his face haggard with grief. "He's gone *tharn*, Jax. Forget it."

Jacqueline wanted to argue, but at that moment, the truck lurched forward with a squeal of rubber. The boy just stood there, unmoving, and the truck plowed into him, burying its grille in the soft flesh of Josh's midsection. He didn't even have time to scream, and amidst the wet tearing sounds, there was a staccato pop as his body bent backwards at an impossible angle. His feet left the ground, and his head flopped back, vacant eyes seeming to accuse Jacqueline and Remy as his torso was shredded and sucked into the truck's digestive mechanism.

Jax felt the insistent tug at her arm, and turned away from the gruesome tableau to see Remy's worried face.

"We've got to go, Jax," he said. "It'll be done in a minute, and then it's coming after us. C'mon!"

She spared one last look back, and she regretted it. Josh had been folded in half, and his arms and legs slapped together as they disappeared in the sticky red mist that now surrounded the truck's fender. She allowed Remy to haul her down the alley, and as they reached the fire escape and began to climb, they heard the truck's horn sound. Its insistent blatting was answered by one, then another from the surrounding area.

Remy and Jax paused two flights up and watched the truck enter the narrow side street. It stopped in the mouth of the alley, and Jax did her best to convince herself that the bright splash of red across its front was just an abandoned paint job. She knew better, of course, but she couldn't bear to think that the crimson stain was all that remained of Josh.

It idled there, and its horn uttered a short bark. An identical response came from the other end of the alley, and Jax and Remy spun around to see the newcomer — a Jeep — roll into place to block the opposite entrance. The truck's horn let out two rapid blats, and it was echoed by the Jeep. Then, the two vehicles rolled toward each other at a snail's pace.

Jax was astonished. "Good Lord," she whispered. "Are they communicating?"

Remy let out a breath, and his face looked old and tired. "More than that, Jax," he said. "They're working together, canvassing the alley for us."

Jax felt a cold wave of despair flood her bones. "That's impossible."

"No," said a new voice, crisp and familiar, from the apartment window behind them. "It's not impossible. They've adapted to the loss of their central neural network. The development of rudimentary communication skills was inevitable."

Jax stifled a shriek as she whirled about and brought her rifle up to bear on the man who was leaning out on the sill.

Austin Malone

Remy reached out a quick hand and shoved the barrel aside. "Don't, Jax," he said in a low voice. "It's him. It's Bachmann."

The old man dipped his mostly bald head in a slow nod of agreement. "That's right, young man. I trust you're the representatives of the gentleman I spoke to earlier this week?"

Jax nodded, opening her mouth to speak, but Bachmann cut her off with a brisk wave of his hand.

"Introductions can wait," he said as he bent to rummage through a bag at his feet. "I have some urgent business to attend to first, and then we can proceed to my laboratory."

Jax peered in at him, and tried to reconcile this man with the Dr. Bachmann she remembered from the BioGreen publicity vids. The Bachmann of her memories was a jovial, robust fellow who had always more resembled Colonel Sanders than he did the typical image of a scientist. Now, less than two years after the disaster, he had lost a lot of weight, as well as most of his hair. Scarecrow-thin, with a cottony fringe of dirty-white hair that ran from above one ear around the back of his head to the other, his appearance did not inspire confidence.

Bachmann straightened, holding a walkie-talkie in one hand and a brown paper bag in the other. With a grunt, he slowly clambered over the windowsill, ending up between Jax and Remy. Leaning over the rail of the fire escape, he glanced down at the vehicles that were inching toward one another. They were still a good two meters apart, and Bachmann nodded to himself.

"Good," he said. "I was afraid all three had come. I really can't afford to destroy all three."

Jax started to laugh at the idea of this pathetic little man taking out two cars, but she caught sight of Remy's wide eyes darting between the walkie-talkie and the bag, and she sobered.

"What's in the bag, Bachmann?" she said.

Bachmann chuckled, but it was Remy who spoke. In a quiet, serious voice, he said, "Jax, I think we should get inside."

With a manic grin, the old man switched on the walkie-talkie and said, "Quite right. I doubt that this flimsy metal staircase will be able to withstand the blast under the weight of all three of us."

Jax felt her jaw unhinge. "Blast?"

Remy grabbed her by the elbow and tugged. "C'mon, Jax, time to go."

She allowed herself to be led through the window and into the apartment. Remy pulled her through its living room and out its front door into the outer hallway before she dug her heels in, demanding to know what the hell was going on.

He shut the door behind them and leaned against it, too much white still showing in his eyes. "Plastique," he said.

"As in plastic explosives? And the walkie-talkie is what, some kind of detonator?"

Remy's head bobbed in a quick nod. "I'm guessing so, yeah. The concept was pretty popular with some of the locals in Afghanistan. They used cell phones to trigger their bombs, but I'd guess the principle is the same with a walkie-talkie. Thread a wire from a turned-off cell into a lump of plastique, leave it in a high traffic area or toss it into a crowd, then dial the number. Kaboom."

Austin Malone

She studied his haunted eyes, starting to get worried herself. "You're actually scared. Why?"

"Because there's no way to know how much explosive he's using, or how potent the stuff is. It could fizzle out, doing about as much damage as a Fourth of July bottle rocket, or..."

"Or?"

He drew in a shuddering breath and met her eyes. "Or it could level the entire block."

She blinked. "Oh."

From the other side of the door, there was a sound like thunder, and Jax and Remy held on to each other as the floor shook beneath their feet. Then, a second later, it was over.

Jax sagged with relief, and Remy pulled her closer into a tight embrace. With her face pressed against his chest, she swallowed the hysterical sobs that threatened to escape, and took deep breaths until the urge to cry had passed.

He rested his chin on top of her head, and stroked her hair. When her trembling subsided, he pulled himself away and looked at her. "You okay?"

She squared her shoulders and nodded. "I so need a vacation after this."

He laughed and reached for the doorknob. "Ready to see what's behind door number one?"

"Let's do it."

He pushed the door open, and the two of them reentered the apartment. The explosion had kicked up dust from every surface, and it hovered at their feet like mist, obscuring the odd spots where the floor now canted, and they clung to each other as they staggered like drunks toward the window.

Austin Malone

The twisted wreckage of the fire escape hung, quivering, in front of the window from which all the glass had been shattered.

"This ain't lookin' good, Jax," Remy muttered.

She snorted. "Ya think?"

Jax stepped forward and leaned out the window, taking care to avoid the shards of glass that still gripped the pane, and when she saw what lay below, she hung her head.

"Dammit," she whispered.

Remy joined her and looked down. The truck had been obliterated. The only thing left intact was a portion of the bed that was now protruding from the mouth of a dumpster twenty feet away. The Jeep, though, looked mostly unharmed, and a skinny pair of legs dangled from its front end over the edge of the crater the bomb had made.

"Wesson's not gonna be happy," Remy said. He looked for a moment longer. Then he gave Jax a pat on the shoulder, and they turned together, heading for the door. But the voice that floated through the window froze them before they had taken more than a couple of steps.

"Haha!" Bachmann's triumphant voice crowed from the alley. "I've got you, you miserable thing!"

Jacqueline spun and looked down to see Bachmann scooting out from under the Jeep with a glowing green tube clutched in one fist. The old man fiddled with some wires that protruded from the end of the tube, and the reaction was intense. The canister brightened, and with static popping noises, green sparks began to spray from the end.

Austin Malone

Bachmann got to his feet and took off in a sprint, holding the crackling cylinder aloft like a geriatric Olympic torch-bearer.

Jax shook her head, puzzled. "What is he doing?"

Remy tugged her back into the apartment. "Beats me, but we'd better follow him. The energy output of that battery pack is going to draw every car in the neighborhood after him." He cursed as they hit the front door and headed down the landing to the street. "Crazy old bastard is making our little search-and-rescue mission really difficult."

They exited the building just in time to see the old man rounding the corner a block to their left. Jax stepped off the curb to follow, but Remy grabbed her by the fabric of her knapsack and hauled her back as a car, a black low-slung sports model, roared past in pursuit of the old man.

"Jesus," she gasped.

"Just watch where you're going, huh?" Remy snapped. "I refuse to go back home empty-handed."

She gulped and looked both ways before stepping into the street this time. Remy fished out a concussion grenade, and he exchanged a fierce glance with her before running toward the corner around which Bachmann and the car had disappeared.

Jax ran after him in a sideways gait, keeping an eye on the street behind them, and holding her spike strip tube at the ready. She nearly plowed into Remy at the intersection when he came to an abrupt halt. "The hell?" he muttered.

Jax peered over his shoulder and was just as perplexed by what she saw. Bachmann had diverted from the street and entered a small public park. With the devastation that lay all around, with residences and businesses in ruins, it was strange to see playground equipment standing unscathed in the middle of a park. Stranger still was the spectacle of Bachmann dangling from the monkey bars, his stick-thin legs kicking in the air. There was no sign of the car that had chased him, although Jax could still hear the threatening rumble of its engine.

Bachmann twisted to glare at them over one shoulder. "Well, don't just stand there," he yelled. "Help me down!"

Jax and Remy jogged toward the playground, and as they drew nearer, they saw what had happened to the car. Snarling and grinding its gears, it jolted back and forth in a futile attempt to escape the pit that Bachmann had dug for it underneath the bars.

Recognizing the forethought and physical labor that must have gone into the execution of the trap, Jax felt a new sense of respect for Bachmann as she reached out and helped Remy ease him to solid ground.

The instant his feet touched ground, Bachmann let out a whoop and danced a triumphant jig, shaking his fists skyward. "Got you, my little beauty," he sang at the car in the pit. "But don't you worry, precious, you'll be out again soon enough, and then you can lead all of your friends to a watery grave."

Jax shook her head. "You're letting it out? But how? And what do you mean, watery grave?"

Bachmann turned his maniacal grin upon her. "All in good time, my dear. Now, if you would be so kind, there's a toolbox on top of the slide over there. Fetch it for me, if you please." Then, to Remy, he added, "There's also a shovel underneath the slide. I'm afraid there's only the one, so you and the young lady can take turns if you like."

Austin Malone

Remy stared at him for a beat and then shrugged and joined Jax at the slide. He raised his eyebrows at her and jerked his head in Bachmann's direction.

She reached into the short tunnel on top of the slide and groped around, saying, "We follow his lead, for now. He may be batshit crazy, but we just watched him drop three cars in the space of about five minutes. I like our odds with him. Besides," she said as her fingers snagged the handle of the toolbox and she tugged it onto the chute of the slide, "aren't you just dying to know what his mysterious plan is?"

Remy smiled, but there was a malevolent glint in his eyes. "You bet, Jax. But if he doesn't come out with it soon, I'm tossing him in with his little pet there, and we're going back home."

Jax scowled. "Spoilsport."

Remy's smile broadened to a grin, and he bent to pick up the shovel. They walked back to Bachmann together, and as they approached him, Jax held out the toolbox by its nylon strap and wiggled it.

"So, what's the plan?" she asked.

"Ah. Good," said Bachmann, looking up. "Young man, if you'll look to your right, you'll see a marker."

Remy glanced that way. "You mean the bumper-car flag?"

The old man nodded. "That's right. Start digging there, in an incline toward the pit. We want a ramp. Now, young lady, my toolbox, if you please?"

Jax drew her arm back, jerking the toolbox out of his reach. "Nope," she said. "I said, 'what's the plan?' Telling him to dig, and then asking for your toolbox, is not a plan."

Bachmann frowned and lunged forward, snatching the toolbox from Jacqueline's hands. "The plan," he said, "is for you and your friend to dig a ramp so that once I've overridden the car's sensory input database, I'll be able to drive it out of the pit."

"And then?" Jax prompted.

Bachmann opened the box and withdrew what looked like a cranial saw. "And then, we return to my laboratory where I fit our little friend here with the amplified beacon I've designed."

Jax shook her head. "I don't understand."

Bachmann chuckled. "Remember the story of The Pied Piper? This car is going to be our flute. Come on, I'll explain the rest while we work."

He stood at the edge of the pit, gauging the distance, and then hopped down onto the roof of the car. Jax motioned to Remy, and he shouldered the shovel without a word and headed for the marker.

The sun was low on the horizon by the time they finished, and the black sports car trundled up the ramp with Bachmann behind its wheel. Despite his reassurances, Jax and Remy kept themselves well away from the car's front end as they piled in with their gear. Thankful to be off of their feet for the first time in what seemed like days, the pair dozed while Bachmann steered them toward the amusement park.

Jacqueline's shallow nap was interrupted when she felt the car come to a stop, and she heard the click-creak of the driver-side door opening as Bachmann got out. She toyed with the idea of waking up all the way, but the steady rhythm of Remy's soft snoring lulled her back under.

Austin Malone

After a few minutes, unfamiliar sounds disturbed her slumber again, and she drifted close enough to consciousness to open her eyes. Bachmann's narrow ass was inches away from her face, and a variety of whirring and clicking noises arose from where his upper half was engaged with the tangle of wires that now hung from beneath the steering column. She screwed her eyes shut and went back to sleep.

Some time later, Jax felt the sensation of movement, and she woke again to find that they were no longer on the midway. Bachmann was parking the car in front of a squat, grey building that glowed with a dull luster in the moonlight. Next to her, Remy's jaw cracked as he yawned.

After bringing the car to a stop, Bachmann swiveled in his seat to look at Remy. "Well, young man. This is it, the spillway control center. You'll find my notebook with the prompt codes next to the command console. Remember to wait for my signal before initiating the process. I want to be sure we get as many of them as we can."

Remy lifted a hand to his forehead in a salute and opened the door to get out. After unfolding himself and stretching in the cool night air, he flashed a grin at Jax in the back seat and said, "See you in a few hours."

Jax waved, and Bachmann waited until Remy disappeared into the building before putting the car in drive and pulling away. From the control center, they took the service bridge across the river, and Jacqueline directed Bachmann to her community's main tunnel entrance, marveling at how quickly they were able to make the trip by car. She had almost forgotten how convenient it was to drive.

As she got out of the car, she made one last appeal to Bachmann. "I don't understand why you have to put yourself down there, too. Can't you just, I dunno, push the car into the drainage canal?"

He gave her a tired, gentle smile and shook his head. "I would if I could, my dear, but the equipment I've cobbled together is too delicate. I can't risk it getting dislodged as our little friend goes careening to the bottom of the culvert. Run along, now, and tell your people what's about to happen. If it works, I've included the schematics for the beacon in that notebook that your friend now has in his possession. Maybe some bright young man or woman of yours will be able to improve upon my design and help other survivors elsewhere, eh?"

Jax gulped and felt the sting of tears. "So this is it, then?"

"I'm afraid so, Jacqueline. With any luck, this will help to redeem my memory. Take care."

"Goodbye," she whispered, and she shut the car door.

She saw his silhouette through the slightly-tinted window bend to adjust something beneath the dashboard, and a sudden surge of dizziness overtook her as the beacon's subsonic discharge rolled off the car. Then, with a final wave, he piloted the vehicle away, back toward the drainage culvert.

As the twin red dots of Bachmann's taillights dwindled in the distance, members of her commune poured out of the main portal, assaulting her with shouted questions. She shook herself out of her sleep-deprived melancholy and began issuing orders.

"Sound the alarms! Which ones? All of 'em. We need everyone topside. Evacuate the tunnels, double-time! Go!"

"What about the cars?" someone shouted.

Austin Malone

"I'll toss you to them if you don't follow orders," she snarled. "Are you deaf? Those tunnels are about to flood. We need everyone out!"

Even as klaxons and sirens began to sound, Jax saw the first of the cars in the distance. A pair of headlights a few blocks over was soon joined by another, then another, and soon there were dozens of them. The growing crowd gasped and muttered as the vehicles rolled past, sedate and heedful only of the siren call of the beacon.

Some cars trundled past close enough to be touched, but no one dared risk the requisite limb. A short time later, their numbers declined, and heavy traffic dwindled to a handful of lone stragglers. Then, there were no more headlights, and silence and darkness blanketed the city.

"What happens now, Ms. Marx?"

It was Sandra, gazing up at Jax with anxious eyes.

Jax smiled. "It's a surprise, hon."

At that moment, the silence was split by a high-pitched screech, as the first of Bachmann's rockets went up. The crack of thunder ripped across the sky, and a brilliant blossom of red light unfolded from the blackness. More followed, and the fireworks that Bachmann had stuffed in the car's trunk lit the night sky and the land below with their multihued explosions.

Jax imagined Remy watching the pyrotechnics from Springfield and initiating the sequence that would open the floodgates, and the colored lights blurred in her vision. She gave her eyes a quick self-conscious swipe, but she stopped when she looked around and saw the tears streaming freely down the cheeks of her friends and adopted family members.

Austin Malone

While she knew that they had no idea what the dazzling display signified on this night, she felt the visceral tug of emotion that the fireworks inspired. Regardless of the occasion, fireworks had always been an expression of celebration, of triumph, and of hope. She saw those sentiments reflected in dozens of pairs of glistening eyes, and she grinned, allowing herself to be swept away by that tidal surge of emotion.

The last rocket exploded, leaving its afterimage seared upon the retinas of the onlookers, and the booming of fireworks was transplanted by a deep groaning sound from the direction of the causeway. The distant roaring susurration that followed elicited a cheer from Jacqueline's people. It was a good sound, a perfect complement to that of the river being diverted from its course, and Jax drank it in, filling her ears with the song of her city's freedom.

Austin Malone

A Fancy Dinner Party

Leo King

Lord Henry Winchester was a very reasonable man.

He always wore sensible clothing befitting a gentleman, opened the door for the ladies, and paid his taxes on time each year. He always kept abreast of local and regional politics and made sure to support the candidate with the most moderate, reasonable platform. While out in public, he made sure to walk with pride, tip his top hat to passersby, and give the local constables a polite, "Good morning."

Even after the global pandemic and catastrophic crop failure that wiped out ninety percent of the world's food supply while leaving the human population untouched, Lord Winchester remained a reasonable man. He would ration out his food, donate to the local shelter, and actively support Parliamentary legislation that would solve the rapidly rising food crisis.

And in the summer of 2055, when Parliament passed the "Comestibles Proposition Act," thus establishing "meat lottery," Lord Winchester openly supported the legislation, even going so far as to volunteer to be the Head Butcher for the Ealing district of London, his home borough. Once appointed that position, he went about his job with pride, working closely with the lads at the Selection Center to sort through the eligible candidates, send out the Butchers to retrieve them, and send the meat to the processing plant in Park Royal.

Of course, there was opposition. After all, no one wants to be butchered, much less eaten, but the Comestibles Proposition Act was passed by necessity. The animals that had survived the pandemic, such as canines, felines, and rodents, were so riddled with disease that consuming them was as risky to one's health as not eating at all.

By the time Parliament passed the Comestibles Proposition Act, their only other choices were to let the population starve to death, allow disease to run rampant like it did in France and Germany due to eating rodents, or allow the entire infrastructure to fall into anarchy as it had in the United States.

Lord Winchester was very glad that England's elected officials had chosen the sensible route.

Early in his tenure as Head Butcher of Ealing, Lord Winchester realized that reasonability and sensibility were even more paramount than before.

When his first several hundred intakes were met with opposition, with more than a tolerable share of Butchers returning with bloody noses and gaping stab wounds, Lord Winchester approached Parliament with a proposed solution – to make the Comestibles Proposition Act the "in" thing.

And so over the next few years, Parliament put forth a massively successful propaganda campaign promoting the Comestibles Proposition Act. Scientists were paraded in front of the general public, touting the advantages of eating human flesh. Anthropologists were brought on daytime talk shows to herald the positives of embracing cannibalism.

Celebrity chefs, such as the famous Nathaniel Abernathy, author of the 2057 best-selling *1001 Recipes for Aunt Gertrude*, delivered popular recipes for meat from the processing plant. And even superstar model Diane Henderson, best known for winning the gold medal in Figure Skating in the 2058 Winter Olympics, promoted the Act, coining the phrase, "Just Be Glad It's Not You."

So by the summer of 2065, everyone in England, from the young to the old, embraced the Comestibles Proposition Act and all that it entailed. Citizens would even assist Butchers in locating any unpatriotic person-ages that tried to flee once their name was posted on the internet by the Selection Center, and there was talk about allowing volunteers to come forward during quarterly collection times in exchange for immunity for their family for an entire year.

For his efforts, Lord Winchester was knighted, given the title "Lord of Ealing," and offered the position of Prime Minister, which he politely refused, saying that, as a reasonable man, he was happy just to serve his country. His humility and virtue were rewarded with the position of Grand Butcher of Londonshire, the high-est position under the Comestibles Proposition Act, as well as a hefty pension and lifetime immunity from the Selection Center for his entire household.

"Gerald," called Lord Winchester from his dressing closet as he compared cuff links to the shade of his din-ner shirt, "have you seen my solid gold pocket watch? I want to wear it this evening."

Gerald, Lord Winchester's stiff-lipped butler whose head was always tilted upwards as if he were catching the tail end of the foulest smell, strolled into his master's room. He said, "Sir, I do believe it is still at the watchmaker's. If you recall, the main spring had gotten a bit... springy... over the past few months."

"Of course it's springy," said Lord Winchester with a grin, deciding on the gold cuff links with ruby attachments over the silver ones with sapphires. "It's a spring, isn't it?"

"Very observant of you, sir," Gerald replied dryly. "Shall I go retrieve the silver pocket watch your Aunt Marceline got you for Christmas?"

"No," replied Lord Winchester as he compared bowties, finally deciding on the one that was the same red hue as his cuff links. "It will clash with my cuff links. Instead..." He held out his bowtie. "Say, Gerald, be a good man and tie this for me."

As Gerald tied the bowtie, Lord Winchester continued, "I will just go without. After all, I am hosting the dinner party tonight. I don't think a small slip of etiquette will cause that much of a fuss?"

"Doubtful, sir," was Gerald's droll reply as he finished the bowtie.

Turning back to his mirror, Lord Winchester said, "Good, then, Gerald. That's all for now. See to the dinner preparations, will you?"

With a "very good, sir," Gerald left his master alone to finish preparing.

For the past ten years, Lord Henry Winchester had been hosting an annual dinner party for his closest friends, though the list changed occasionally due to selections. It was considered to be one of the highest social honors to be invited to Lord Winchester's annual dinner party, and throughout the year, he received considerable favors and, in some cases, outright bribes, to be placed on the list.

Of course, Lord Winchester never put anyone on the guest list just because of their gifts to him over the course of the year, for after all, he was a reasonable man who saw such actions as crass and uncivilized.

So after finishing his dressing, Lord Winchester headed downstairs to go over the final preparations for the party and then to wait for his guests.

Even though his home was modeled in the fashion of the late Victorian, it had all the modern conveniences of the middle twenty-first century. The air conditioning automatically adjusted the temperature based on the body heat in the room, the entire house was wired with a state-of-the-art sound system, and the lights, which were all artificial sunlight, gave the interior a comfortable glow about it. Lord Winchester loved his home, and he managed its staff with fairness and equanimity.

Entering the kitchen, he was greeted by the smell of stew with rosemary. It was a simply scrumptious and savory scent, and he approached the stove where the large aluminum pot was bubbling, eager for a peek. His cook, Pierre Crosier, who had been standing nearby and instructing a new kitchen boy on the proper manner of garnishing plates, turned and greeted him with his obnoxiously French accent.

"Ah, *Monsieur* Winchester," said Pierre, clapping his hands together, "you are here to see how things are going, *oui*?"

"Yes, Pierre," replied Lord Winchester with a cordial smile, "are the preparations nearly complete?"

"*Oui oui*," Pierre replied ardently, making a sweeping motion that invited his master to tour the kitchen. "As you can see, the stew, the potatoes, and the rice, they are all ready. We are just waiting on the dessert."

Leo King

Of course, by comparison to starving to death, a bowl of Millicent Soup or Leg of Bertie is a sumptuous feast, so Lord Winchester's menus, especially with such rare ingredients as rice, were among the most extravagant to be found in Great Britain.

"Marvelous," replied Lord Winchester as he began to walk about the kitchen. Everything seemed to be in order, with the kitchen boys and assistant cooks working hard to prepare the meal. Stopping near the exit to the dining room, he looked at his cook and asked, "What is for dessert again, Pierre?"

"Ah," Pierre replied, again clapping his hands together, "this evening, we have a freshly baked Irish cream pie."

Lord Winchester couldn't help but grin again, and asked, "So then, are there any Irish in it?"

Pierre laughed at the joke as if it were the funniest thing the world, and with a polite nod to his cook, Lord Winchester left for the dining room.

There, Gerald was overseeing the placement of the dinnerware and glasses from the head to the foot of the twelve-foot table. Lord Winchester silently counted out the spaces - twelve places for eleven guests plus himself. Everything was perfect.

"Good job, Gerald," Lord Winchester said as he headed out of the dining room and into the main hall. "I'll be in my study getting some work done. Do come and fetch me when the first guests arrive."

"Very good, sir," replied Gerald, who then turned to correct a maid's folding of a napkin.

Entering his study, which was so antiquated as to look a hundred years out of place, Lord Winchester sat at his desk.

With the tap of a finger, he activated a button underneath the desk, and on the far wall, a bookcase slid back, revealing a large monitor. Once it turned on, revealing his email inbox, Lord Winchester said, "Sort mail by priority. Open first mail."

"Your mail has been sorted," replied the computer's voice, which Lord Winchester had configured to sound like early twenty-first-century actor Stephen Fry. "First message is from Prime Minister York. Do you wish to hear it?"

"Yes," replied Lord Winchester, sitting back and checking his notes for the month. Selection had hit a difficult point two quarters ago, with many families in the West End and Knightsbridge finding legal loopholes to gain temporary immunity. Luckily, Parliament had passed an update to legislation that closed those loopholes, ensuring that only those who directly served England or had family members who volunteered for selection that quarter could be granted any sort of immunity.

"Henry," began the Prime Minister's email, read to him in the same Stephen Fry voice, "give us a call tomorrow, after your dinner party. The lads and I want to go over those numbers for the rural boroughs. We think there is a census error. Also, we need to get ready for the next general election. I suspect that prat Martin is going to try a name-smearing campaign. Can't have that. Cheerio, mate!"

Lord Winchester laughed and shook his head, muttering, "Shouldn't have called his wife a bloated, bacteria-ridden gas bag... mate."

"Next message is from your mother," said his computer. "Do you want to hear it?"

Eager to leave Prime Minister York and his constant threat of political usurpers behind, Lord Winchester replied that he did.

"Henry," began the next email, "it's your mother. Is this thing recording? Oh, I hate this. I remember back in the good old days when you typed your emails on a keyboard and blogged on your cellphone. Did you know, Henry, that the scientists at Oxford are on the verge of releasing a chip that will let you dictate emails with your brain? Your brain, Henry! I'm telling you, if not for the food shortage slowing humanity down, we'd all be robots by now. Mark my words."

The voice, which had gotten consistently more frantic over the course of the email, suddenly calmed down. "Anyway, Henry, it's your mother. Your father and I are doing well over here in Wales. We want to come visit you for Christmas. Give us a call soon, all right? Love you, dear! End email. Send email. Wait, is this still recording? Oh, what the bloody—"

Lord Winchester, who had been chuckling during his mother's email, was laughing out loud at the end of it. Shaking his head, he said, "Put a reminder to call Mother next Wednesday at five thirty."

"Schedule updated," said his computer. "Next message is from Mister Corbin at the Ealing District Butcher Shop. Do you want to hear it?"

Lord Winchester knew what that message was about. Ealing District had been having a bit of a problem with anonymous dissidents attacking Butchers on their way home. It was a problem that would spring up for a bit, cause some concern, and then get squelched. But it always put the lads in a terrible temper.

"No," replied Lord Winchester. There was a knock on the door, prompting him to say, "Come in, please."

Gerald opened the door and said, "Sir, Madam Shrewsbury, Lord Farnsworth, and Lord Hillshire, with guest, are here."

"Wonderful," said Lord Winchester, clicking the button under his desk to make his bookcase slide back into place. Getting up and heading to the drawing room to receive his guests, he told Gerald, "See to it that dinner is on time this year. And make sure all the instruments are ready. I don't want any embarrassing delays."

"Of course, sir," replied Gerald with a bow that almost brought his nose to level for a moment.

Lord Winchester, upon entering the drawing room, was greeted by Lord Hillshire, his closest friend, an older gentleman dressed in a military uniform. He had gray mutton chops and ruddy cheeks and looked like the sort of fellow who would have a cheerful disposition. On his arm was a very attractive woman who was no more than twenty years old and looked as out of place in her white dress as a nun in a hatchery.

"Good to see you, Henry, old boy," bellowed Lord Hillshire, clapping Lord Winchester on his arm with evident fondness. "How go things, you old prick? It's been, what, six months?"

Rubbing his arm, then offering his best friend a handshake, Lord Winchester nodded his head. "Almost seven. Since Christmas. Where have you been?"

"Overseas," mused Lord Hillshire, shaking his head disdainfully. "Nasty bit of business in the South Americas right now. Trying to get even a bit of export down there is next to impossible. What's the point of having sky fortresses that can carry acres of coffee beans if there are no coffee beans to carry?"

Frowning, Lord Winchester shook his head. "I am terribly sorry to hear that, old chap. Next time, perhaps?"

"Perhaps," replied Lord Hillshire, who wrinkled his nose and then, covering it at the last moment, sneezed. A moment later, he apologized. "Sorry about that, old chap, this cybernetic nose is giving me all kinds of trouble."

Lord Winchester couldn't help but smirk. "Well, you know what they say, old bean, you live with your choices."

"Har har," Lord Hillshire faux-laughed, and then, as if suddenly remembering that he had a woman on his arm, suddenly shook said arm. The young woman looked about, a bit shocked, and then smiled at both men.

"This," said Lord Hillshire, motioning to the woman with his head, "is Cathy."

"Cassie," replied the young woman in an obvious cockney accent. "I already done corrected you a million times."

"Oh, hush, you," Lord Hillshire retorted. He turned back to his friend to say, "She's not much in conversation, but she's a hellion in bed, old chap!"

Lord Winchester just smiled pleasantly at his best friend, as well as his guest. Hillshire was known to go after those of a lower class. They were the only types he could bed, given that his assets were all monetary.

"So whatever happened to Lily?" Lord Winchester asked, remembering that Hillshire's lady friend at Christmas was a stretch more educated than the rest.

"Selected, sadly," said Lord Hillshire in a downcast tone. "I told her she had to come with me to be immune, but the silly girl wanted to stay with her sick mother.

She was the only bread-winner in the house. Wanted to make sure her mother had enough to eat."

"Well," replied Lord Winchester in a reasonable and emphatic tone, "I'm sure she did just that."

"Yes, yes," muttered his friend, who then led Cassie over to a set of photos of him and Lord Winchester playing tennis in Wimbledon Stadium.

Lord Winchester took his cue to move onto his next guests. Madam Shrewsbury sat on the sofa, fanning herself with an old fan, while her nephew, Lord Farnsworth, stood near an unlit fireplace reading a small booklet. Both were dressed in lavishly expensive, formal dining clothes. As Lord Winchester approached the older lady, she stood, offering her hand to him in greeting.

"Madam Shrewsbury." Lord Winchester greeted her with a kiss of her hand. "Welcome, as always."

"And always nice to see you," replied Madam Shrewsbury, her posture and poise impeccable, as one would expect from the wife of the previous Prime Minister.

"Thank you again for having us at this wonderful dinner party."

"The pleasure, madam," replied Lord Winchester, "is all mine."

Bowing her head just a bit, Madam Shrewsbury turned to look at her nephew, who was still deeply engrossed in his reading material. "Brandon," she said sharply, "will you please put that thing away and come say hello to your host?"

With a start, Lord Farnsworth looked up from his booklet. Lord Winchester saw the word "Derby" on it and knew what it was – a betting booklet for the Derby. Although he disapproved of the young man's gambling habits, he said nothing, only smiling at his guest. After all, no reasonable man would pass judgment on another like that.

"A pleasure to see you again, Lord Winchester," said Lord Farnsworth with an open hand, his cordial smile and gentle demeanor belying his gambling addiction.

"Always a pleasure, Lord Farnsworth," replied Lord Winchester, shaking the young man's hand. "How is that left hand of yours? No problems?"

Bending his wrist a few times, Lord Farnsworth smiled at his host and nodded with enthusiasm. "It's working very well. I almost don't realize it's cybernetic. I have to admit, I am very pleased. So much so, I was thinking of removing my right one, so my left wouldn't get lonely."

Madam Shrewsbury gasped and slapped her nephew with her fan. "Brandon Farnsworth! If your mother could hear you, she'd have a heart attack!"

With a small laugh, Lord Winchester replied, "I find it amusing, Madam Shrewsbury. Your nephew's jovial attitude gives me reason to believe that the youth of our great country can make do once we are departed."

"That's poppycock, and you know it, Winchester," came a crotchety, crackling voice behind him. Lord Winchester, still smiling, turned to see a wizened old prune of a man in a black tuxedo walking up with a walking cane. His head and face were completely bald and he had a look so sour, it was like honey from Eden wouldn't be sweet enough for him.

"Old Man Witherspoon," called Lord Hillshire from the side of the room. "Well, I'll be damned, you old cock, you're here early for once."

"Oh, stuff a sock in your bum, Hillshire," crackled Old Man Witherspoon as he turned to shake Lord

Winchester's hand. "Good to see you and all that. How's the work coming along? Kill anyone today?"

Lord Winchester couldn't feel insulted by Old Man Witherspoon. Everyone knew that the old man was half-senile, bitter with old age, and so filled with artificial organs that he could hardly be considered human. But he was Queen Mary the Second's older brother and had practically raised Lord Winchester, so as far as he was concerned, the old man could say whatever he wanted to him.

Madam Shrewsbury watched with interest, fanning herself, while her nephew went back to reading his Derby book.

"No," replied Lord Winchester with a pleasant smile, shaking Old Man Witherspoon's hand. "I don't actually collect anyone, and you know that. I just oversee the operation."

"Of course," replied Old Man Witherspoon with a snort. "It's only your Butchers who go out and do the dirty work." Turning to Lord Hillshire, and motioning to Cassie with his cane, he added, "And that's a new one, right? She knows what's up, right?"

Lord Hillshire flushed and sidled up to Old Man Witherspoon. "I beg your pardon, sir. Miss Cassie is my lady friend, and yes, she knows what's up. Why wouldn't she?"

"Yes, sir," replied Cassie, who then reached over and tickled Lord Hillshire underneath his chin. "Hillsie-Willsie explained it all to me last night. It's fine with me."

"Is it now," said Old Man Witherspoon with an arched brow. He turned back to Lord Winchester and demanded, "Where do you keep your brandy?"

Leo King

A hand on the back of his old friend, Winchester showed him to the bar and poured him a sizable glass of brandy. He was just getting the old man settled when he saw a flash of sky blue out of the corner of his eye. He drew in a quick breath as he turned to see the angelic visage of the Lady Cromwell.

"Lord Winchester," said Lady Cromwell as he glided across the room to her. "Thank you for having me."

"And thank you for coming, Lady Cromwell," replied Lord Winchester, taking the woman's dainty gloved hand into his own and kissing the top of it tenderly. He had always favored this lovely lady, but, alas, she was half his age and had made it clear that she wouldn't consider him. Looking to her side, he saw a man with a black pencil-thin mustache, looking very proud to be there, smiling at him and nodding his head.

"This," replied Lady Cromwell with a soft exhale, "is my new friend, Lord Brockenshire."

Before Lord Winchester could say anything, Lord Brockenshire thrust his hand toward him, saying, "I have always wanted to meet you, Lord Winchester. It's a pleasure. A real pleasure."

Although Lord Winchester was taken aback, he quickly recovered and, shaking his guest's hand, replied, "The pleasure is all mine, sir. I'm glad to see that Lady Cromwell has such an... enthusiastic guest."

Silently studying Lord Brockenshire's countenance, Lord Winchester wondered how long he should wait before slipping the man's name to the lads at the Selection Center. Feeling that this one was more likely to try to take liberties with Lady Cromwell, he decided on giving it three weeks to a month.

Lord Winchester didn't want to rob Lady Cromwell of any happiness. He was very fond of her, and he wanted her to enjoy her gentleman friends for as long as the relationship was appropriate.

After all, Lord Winchester was a reasonable man.

Once Lady Cromwell had arrived, Lord Winchester got Lord Hillshire to entertain the gathering with one of his stories from abroad. After softening his best friend up with a glass of whiskey, Lord Winchester gave him the stage.

Lord Hillshire took to it like a Shakespearean actor, spinning a bit of a yarn about the situation down in South America, the conflict between the British Commonwealth and the Colombian Empire, and how the brave men and woman of the Royal Air Force's 106th Squadron saved the day with a cruise missile assault on Bogota.

By the time Lord Hillshire had finished his tale, the remaining four guests had arrived: Lord Bigsley, President of the Bank of London, Doctor Blessington and his wife, Sybil, and celebrity chef Nathaniel Abernathy.

With everyone assembled, and Lord Hillshire intoxicated enough that he was threatening to sing, Lord Winchester had everyone move to the dining room.

"Ah, yes," sighed a contented Lord Hillshire as he slurped on the stew, a particularly large chunk of meat sliding off his spoon and back into the broth below. "I do believe that Pierre has outdone himself this time."

"Well, all the credit can't go to Pierre," replied a grateful Lord Winchester, who was ever so politely sipping red wine from a crystal goblet. "He did use a variant on Master Abernathy's succulent recipe for Welsh stew."

"Of course, of course," replied Abernathy, who was clean shaven and dressed in a fancy white coat and tails with blue accents, "my Welsh stew *has* gained national recognition as the one of the heartiest meals during the cold of winter. But, Lord Winchester, you said a variant?"

"Yes, quite," replied Lord Winchester, putting down his goblet to explain. "It's more of a Yorkshire stew actually, since there isn't any Welsh in it."

"Ah, ha," Lord Hillshire merrily roared out, "so it's got Yorkshireman in it! I thought it tasted a bit dense!"

And everyone had a bit of a laugh.

"It's good to hear a Yorkshire joke, Lord Hillshire," replied Lord Farnsworth, who had since abandoned his Derby book in favor of a bit of socializing with the other dinner guests. "After all, if we were too formal, I believe we'd be as stiff as the stiff in the stew."

There was a little snickering from Lord Hillshire, while Madam Shrewsbury shook her head sadly.

"My dear young Farnsworth," replied Old Man Witherspoon, "was that a joke, or did you just announce your candidacy for 'Ass of the Year'?"

While several of the guests chuckled at that, Lady Cromwell spoke up, flittering her eyes toward a rather deeply blushing Lord Farnsworth. "I thought it was rather funny. I mean, we *are* eating someone. Why stand on ceremony?"

"Quite right," replied Lord Winchester, gallantly standing by his favorite lady's side, "we upper class do a spot-on job of pretending that this is some cow or calf that was butchered, but let us never forget the noble sacrifice of the person who is providing this fabulous meal for us tonight."

Lord Winchester raised his glass. "To the Yorkshireman!"

"To the Yorkshireman," replied the guests. Glasses clanked and wine was drunk.

"All this talk of eating people," said Lord Bigsley from beneath his foot-long mustache, "reminds me how far we, as a society, have come this past decade."

There was general nodding as the old banker continued, "I mean, ten years ago, if someone had told me I'd be eating a chap from Yorkshire, I'd call them daft, and then ring the bobbies for them."

"Aye, agreed," replied Abernathy, drumming his fingers thoughtfully on the side of his bowl. "It shows a strong sense of cultural solidarity that we Brits are choosing survival over an ill-conceived notion of morality. After all, isn't it human nature to kill or be killed, eat or be eaten?"

While several of the guests nodded in approval, Doctor Blessington, who had been silent for the majority of the dinner, finally spoke up. The bearded gentleman, dressed in a black suit and wearing spectacles, said, "Well, Master Abernathy, it's far greater than mere human nature."

This comment seemed to get the attention of most of the guests, and even Lord Brockenshire, who was carefully examining the blush an inch above Lady Cromwell's bosom, turned his attention to the good doctor.

"You see," began Doctor Blessington, as he took a moment to pat his mouth dry, "the animals, such as the squirrel, the pig, and even our cousin the chimpanzee, engage in cannibalism on a filial level. That is to say, they devour the young of their enemies, or their young who are otherwise too weak to survive. So, for animals, the act of eating their own kind is more of a Darwin tactic than anything else."

As the guests, for the most part, nodded in comprehension, Doctor Blessington continued, "But humans are different. We are the only species that can not only actively choose to engage in cannibalism, but create an unbiased system of selection.

"In older times, societies in places such as the Amazon Basin and the South Pacific practiced cannibalism as a cultural, and in some cases, religious, ritual. And now, today, we have turned it into a civilized and methodical way to survive as a species."

Reaching for his wine glass, Doctor Blessington concluded, "In that regard, we have risen above our base animal instincts and have embraced cannibalism in its purest, dare I say most divine, form."

As the good doctor sipped his wine, Lord Hillshire, who had gotten rather piss-faced, raised his glass and said, "I'll drink to that. Very well said, Doctor!"

Several other guests raised their glasses to the doctor as well, while Lord Winchester just sat back and smiled pleasantly.

There were some finer points that he didn't necessarily agree with, but he found Doctor Blessington's treatise to be reasonable enough, and so he could not dispute it.

"I'll say one thing," replied Sybil Blessington, a plain-looking older woman who looked as much like her husband's sister as his wife, "the system of selection is frightfully efficient." She turned to Lord Winchester. "Do you mind if I ask you how it works?"

"Oh, come now, dear," retorted Doctor Blessington. "Lord Winchester doesn't want to talk about work at the dinner table."

"It's all right," replied Lord Winchester pleasantly. "It's something I'm always asked by new guests, and I don't mind explaining it."

Lord Hillshire, who looked like he had heard this story a hundred times, returned to getting the attention of a servant to address his criminally empty wine glass, while Madam Shrewsbury, who was the only person who had yet to finish her stew, looked as if she were tuning the conversation out entirely.

Paying no mind to the understandable disengagement of his two longest-running guests, Lord Winchester said, "It works like this: all persons between the ages of sixteen and fifty have their names entered into the mainframe at the Selection Center. Immunity is only granted to the families of those currently serving in Parliament, those who have a family member volunteer for selection, or members of the Royal Family.

"The names are coded into a set of numbers, for security reasons, and entered into a database. Every quarter, each shire and each district has a set of numbers selected. The chance of being selected is approximately one in ten thousand. Those numbers are decoded into names and addresses, and sent to each Butcher's Office. The Butchers then take the names and collect the meat."

"In fact, you mean the *people*, don't you?" replied Sybil Blessington.

"Yes, of course," replied Lord Winchester. "My apologies. That is a crass term used by my department."

"It's quite all right there," assured Abernathy. "After all, they inevitably become just that, meat."

Leo King

As Lord Winchester nodded to Abernathy, Cassie asked, "So, Lord Winchester, how are the people, the meat, um…"

"Oh, come on, now," belched out a rather sloshed, yet still quite merry, Lord Hillshire. "Your one time to speak at dinner, and you ask that?"

As Cassie blushed furiously, Lady Cromwell spoke up. "I think it's a reasonable question. We all wonder it. I know that I do."

"Quite right, we're curious," added Lord Brockenshire, who had gone back to examining the more noticeable assets of his dinner companion.

Doing his best to ignore the brazen behavior of Lord Brockenshire, Lord Winchester turned to Cassie. His smile was gentle. Such questions were encouraged Parliament wanting the general populace to know that there was no pain involved with selection, but as all good British citizens knew, it wasn't good parlor or dinner conversation. But being a reasonable man, he couldn't refuse to answer so honest a question.

"It's very quick," answered Lord Winchester, "and very painless. A quick zip to the back of the neck, and the mea—er, person—just falls down. They never even know it's coming."

"And this is done at the Processing Plant?" asked Cassie.

"Oh, no, my dear Cassie, of course not," replied Lord Winchester, "an abattoir environment produces too much stress, which spoils the meat. No, it's actually done while escorting them to the Butcher Van."

"Interesting," interjected Lord Farnsworth, who had taken a keen interest in the conversation. "So they are dead before they even get loaded up."

"Yes, indeed," replied Lord Winchester. "It's as humane as humanly possible."

"This conversation," said Lord Hillshire, "is killing my buzz, dear friend."

Chuckling, Lord Winchester announced that the conversation could move on if Cassie was satisfied. When the young lady said she was, the air of tension that had been around Lord Hillshire vanished.

"Now, the back alley butcherings," began Lord Farnsworth, "now those are a frightful matter."

A few eyes rolled, and Old Man Witherspoon, who always seemed to enjoy picking on the young noble, crackled out, "Oh for piss' sake, Farnsworth, can't you ever choose an appropriate dinner topic?"

As the young noble blushed furiously, Madam Shrewsbury, who had finished her stew at last, said, "Well, Lord Witherspoon, if you would be so kind as to stop picking on my nephew, he brings up a good point. Lord Winchester," the old woman said, turning to her host, "does your department have any way of controlling those renegades?"

"I'm afraid that's a matter for the police," replied Lord Winchester, who, like all other reasonable men, was disturbed by the recent trend of roving packs of civilians grabbing random people off the street and killing them for black market meat sales. "Personally, of course, the matter disgusts me greatly. After all, I don't approve of murder."

"Hear, hear," replied Bigsley. "Sensible Englishmen do not randomly murder their fellow men and sell them in back alleys. What are we, animals? Americans?"

Lord Hillshire gave such a whooping laugh at Lord Bigeley's comment that half the table jumped. "Now that's a sorry state of affairs. The United States. Did you know," began the epically drunken nobleman, "that they have marauding bands of ruffians who straight up murder entire colonies, slave trafficking centers that see more commerce than nomadic traders, religious cults based on nanotechnology, and a computer that claims to be the President of the United States?"

"My God," replied Sybil Blessington, "how do the Americans live?"

"Like animals," replied Old Man Witherspoon, who sipped his wine with disgust, "like packs of animals."

"So true," added Lord Hillshire. "It's a sad country. A shame, too — I had so wanted to go to Disneyland."

At that comment, the doors to the dining room opened, and in came Pierre with several kitchen boys and girls, all wheeling in trays of covered plates, all in the most beautifully decorated silver with gold inlay. The smell coming from the trays was simply scrumptious.

"Is that rice I smell?" asked Lady Cromwell, her dark, seductive eyes getting a childlike joy about them.

Lord Winchester, who couldn't help but admire those eyes, replied that it was indeed rice.

"A very rare treat," said a very impressed Lord Bigsley. "How did you get it?"

"The horticulture lab is finally able to make a pittance of rice," replied Lord Winchester as Pierre placed his covered plate before him. "I used up my year's ration for tonight."

"Oh, now, you didn't have to do that," said a remarkably impressed Madam Shrewsbury, her smile most genuine. "Really, Henry, you are too much sometimes."

Lord Winchester just gave his most pleasant smile to his guests as their platters were placed in front of each of them.

"My dearest Madam, I would never dream of giving my guests anything but the very best."

As Pierre and the kitchen staff stepped back, Lord Hillshire rose, lifted his glass, and, steadying himself, said, "To all of us, and to you, old chap — I want to thank you for throwing such a *fancy* dinner party. To Lord Winchester!"

"To Lord Winchester," replied the rest of the guests. Glasses clinked and were drained. Lord Winchester just nodded in thanks, too modest to say anything.

The platter covers were lifted, and the sweet aroma of cooked rice wafted throughout the dining room. Each plate had a bed of rice with a garnish of herbs and spices that, like the rice, was artificially grown and therefore exceedingly expensive.

As the kitchen staff set up table-side portable stoves, Pierre lifted Lord Winchester's cover. On his bed of rice was a steaming, well-cooked toe, covered in a white wine sauce.

"Had to go first again, aye, chap?" replied Hillshire with a grin, needling his best friend.

Lord Winchester smiled and nodded. "I need to keep my wits about me, in the case of something going wrong, old friend."

"Well, it won't," said Old Man Witherspoon as he rolled up his left sleeve. "It never does. You're just being a paranoid old coot, Winchester."

With a gentlemanly nod to his eldest guest, Lord Winchester said to his table, "Now, please make sure you inject the local anesthetic just above the cutting point. For you first-timers, I recommend a pinky finger.

As soon as you are done, inject the nano-coagulant directly into the wound. This will stop the bleeding and allow the cyber-doctors to easily put your replacement on. Be sure—"

"Yeah, yeah," stammered out an impatient Lord Hillshire, who snatched the first syringe from the kitchen boy serving him and jammed it into his middle left finger above the third knuckle. "Just watch me, everyone, and I'll show you how to do it."

As Lord Hillshire took the electric knife from the kitchen boy and got to work, Lord Winchester sat back. Like Madam Shrewsbury, his best friend had been to every single one of his annual dinner parties and was as close to a "pro" at the art as one could be.

Lord Winchester didn't mind letting Lord Hillshire have center stage for now. After all, any reasonable man would share the spotlight with his closest friend.

"Lord Winchester," asked Lady Cromwell, who was having Lord Brockenshire inject the local into her right big toe, "this is your last toe this year, isn't it?"

"Sadly," replied Lord Winchester, who motioned for Pierre to assist Old Man Witherspoon, whose difficulty with injecting his finger was causing the old man to loudly proclaim he'd just bite it off.

"Next year, I'll have to work on my fingers. That means I'll have to do it a day in advance. I can't very well host without a cybernetic replacement. But I do so hate frozen meat."

"I am so sorry," replied sympathetic Lady Cromwell, as Lord Brockenshire emerged from under the table with a bloodied big toe; the mess quickly vanished with the injection of the nano-coagulant. "Perhaps you should just take a bit of the calf, or some rib?"

"Or he can cut off a piece of his ass," replied Lord Hillshire with a riotous chortle. "God knows he has a lot of that to spare."

Lord Winchester chuckled and shook his head, watching his best friend, clearly so drunk he nearly took off his entire hand, make a spectacle of himself. Turning to his other guests, he watched as they went through similar motions.

Lord Bigsley had chosen a thumb, and Abernathy went for an ear, while the Blessingtons, after a furious low-volume debate, appeared to agree to help each other with their noses. Lord Farnsworth, after helping his aunt with her left pinkie toe, asked if it would be kosher to choose his pillock.

"Good God, Farnsworth," cackled out Witherspoon, "however will you pee?"

"They have a prosthesis for that," replied a rather noseless Doctor Blessington.

"Ah," said Old Man Witherspoon, a bit surprised. "Well, lop it off, then, son, if that's your itch."

Minutes later, the smell of freshly cooking meat filled the dining room, and pleasant conversation was had. Cassie in particular was surprised at the lack of pain, and she kept looking in amazement at the place where her right pinky used to be, the wound already closing thanks to the nanotechnology.

Lord Winchester just kept smiling and chatting with his guests, finding the good will, even between Lord Farnsworth and Old Man Witherspoon (who seemed to respect the young noble's choice of cut), a refreshing break from work.

Soon, the meat was served, and everyone remarked how delightful the taste was, how the herbs and spices brought out the flavor, and how the wine sauce was impeccable. Abernathy even raised his glass to Pierre, saying that never before had he been served a meal that he felt rivaled his own and that if the French cook ever wanted to appear as a guest on his show, he'd be more than welcome. Pierre wiped away a tear of joy.

When dinner finally ended, dessert was brought, and the Irish cream pie, served with a round of "is there any Irish in it" jokes, was an instant hit. Soon, the guests were retiring to the lounge or the library for some after dinner reading, port, and sherry, as well as conversation As soon as Lord Winchester was situated in his favorite chair in his lounge, he was approached by Lord Bigsley.

"I just wanted to say," said Lord Bigsley, "thank you for inviting me. Ever since my dear Lydia was selected, I admit I felt my conviction toward the British Way wavering. But tonight, realizing the greatest act of enlightenment that a man can have — to consume his own flesh — well, I just feel revitalized."

Lord Winchester smiled, nodded, and shook Lord Bigsley's good hand, saying, "Any reasonable man would understand that this is how we British are now. And you, Lord Bigsley, are a very reasonable man."

Lord Bigsley gave a nod of approval before going off to have a stimulating debate with a glass of brandy.

From his chair, Lord Winchester watched Lady Cromwell and her rogue of a date, Lord Brockenshire, chatting with Lord Farnsworth on some topic of youthful interest. For a moment, sadness filled Lord Winchester's heart, that she would never return his feelings.

She did, however, catch his gaze and give him a pleasant, genuine smile. That made Lord Winchester's evening, and putting aside his own feelings, he continued to play host to his guests until the last one left.

"Another very successful dinner party," said Gerald, folding up Lord Winchester's clothing as his master undressed.

"Indeed," replied Lord Winchester, feeling particularly tired. "I saw some friends I have not seen in many months, and between Lord Bigsley and Dr. Blessington, I believe I have made my social and economic contacts for the year. A very successful evening, if I do say so."

Once undressed except for his skivvies, Winchester sat down and rubbed cream into his feet. The cooling sensation on his aching soles and equally tired toes felt simply amazing.

Looking at his master's feet, Gerald asked, "So, sir, what will you do starting next year? You cannot hide your hands quite so easily."

"I'm not sure," replied Lord Winchester, rubbing sensation back into each exhausted toe, "but I'll think of something. I always do."

"Do you think that they suspect anything?" asked Gerald, a hint of caution to his voice.

"Not at all," replied Lord Winchester, standing up to pull on his nightgown. "They're all so taken in by the rubbish fed to them about eating people that they'd never suspect me of not participating. Thank Pierre, by the way, for the lab-cultured beef in the stew, and making that tofu look like a toe. Masterful work."

"Of course, sir," replied Gerald, taking the dirty clothes with him and turning down the bed for his master. "So long as you have faith we'll not be found out, none of us will worry."

Leo King

As Lord Winchester slid into bed, he gave his loyal butler a reassuring smile. "Relax, Gerald. I just convinced eleven otherwise reasonable people to eat a part of themselves — again. I think I can work out the details for next year's dinner party."

"As you say, sir," replied Gerald, who closed the drapes and turned off the lights. "Have a good night, sir. Sleep well."

"Good night, Gerald," replied Lord Winchester with a yawn as he settled down in bed. As sleep overcame him, he was sure that, so long as he kept his wits about him, he would never ever consume a single ounce of human flesh, much less his own.

After all, Lord Henry Winchester was a very reasonable man.

Heirloom

B.H. Werner

Jesse watched small raindrops patter gently against the window at work. It was a Monday, and the sky was clouded and dark enough that it looked like dusk, even though it was only midday. Normally, Jesse would have loved a day like this. The whole world seemed quieter, and the rolling charcoal grey clouds reminded him of comfortable blankets.

But today, they seemed less comforting and more quietly menacing, making Jesse feel a little claustrophobic. Outside, the very air he breathed seemed determined to suffocate him. It had been uncommonly hot and humid for fall, and every breath of air felt like gulping down water.

Comfortable or not, it seemed like a fitting day for his mother's funeral. Maybe the sky was actually crying and trying to get the attention of everyone who had ignored poor Doreen, who had inexplicably fallen over dead at age 59. Neither Jesse nor Doreen had had an easy go of it with Jesse's father, Walter.

Walter had always treated Jesse with a mix of neglect and emotional abuse, but Jesse knew his mother had gotten the worst of it. Walter routinely got in public fights, and Doreen was always known for wearing heavy makeup. Jesse knew she was covering up after going five rounds with Walter.

Oddly enough, after Walter had died inexplicably a few years earlier, Jesse's mother had seemed even more withdrawn and disturbed. She always had huge bags under her eyes. Jesse had tried to talk to her about it, but she had always forced a smile, insisted everything was fine, and offered to make him some food. In those moments, Jesse wondered how deep a bond a person could form with their abuser.

Jesse's watch beeped and snapped him out of his far-away thoughts. *Lunch time.* He spun his chair around in his cubicle to check his email to see if Kent was going to join him for a bite before he had to go off to the funeral.

Kent was the closest thing Jesse had to a friend. Jesse had always been a little socially awkward; he managed to chase most would-be friends off with stories of his nightmares, which could have easily been made into horror movies. But Kent had been slow to judge. He looked past many of Jesse's quirks, and Jesse had managed to keep his night terrors to himself.

So, a couple of times a week, Kent and Jesse would get lunch together. It usually started with some good-natured back-and-forth and ended with one of them flipping a coin to decide between a few of their regular haunts. But not today.

Kent had been suspiciously quiet on email today, to the point that Jesse had nearly called IT to look into email server problems, but a few inane meeting requests had come through. Jesse shook the mouse to wake up his computer. As the screen warmed up, his throat tightened with anxiety. Had he made a mistake by confiding in Kent?

Jesse had told Kent he had dreamed about his mother dying the day before he got the call that she had actually passed. He hadn't told Kent that she died in his dream because a terrible beast on her back, gnawing at her neck, had reached in and pulled out her heart.

An email from Kent simply titled, "Lunch," sat at the top of Jesse's inbox. He clicked on it with the same callous haste with which you tear off a bandage.

"I can't make it today," was all the email said. No witty pith. No insults about how long Jesse's nose was or how awkwardly he flirted. No jokes about giving up women for barn animals.

The five simple words hit Jesse like a punch in the gut. He grabbed his coat off the back of his chair, put his computer in sleep mode, and strode briskly toward the parking lot with his head down and his eyes on his shoes.

The night of his mother's funeral, it started. Jesse had lived most of his life with nightmares. Terrible ones. Nightmares that would scare hardened prisoners. But tonight, his nightmares began to come to life.

Jesse had been in bed for twenty minutes when he heard an almost inaudible knock from the ceiling. Jesse held his breath, straining to discover if his ears were playing tricks on him. Then a few knocks. He hoped it was a raccoon or some sort of rodent. He'd call the exterminator tomorrow.

But the knocks kept coming louder and faster, until it sounded like some sort of beast was running around in the attic. Jesse hunkered down into his covers, trying to will himself awake. This must be a dream, right? He'd fallen asleep and didn't realize it. It happened all the time.

Jesse pinched himself. It hurt, but that didn't necessarily mean anything. His dreams were intense. A huge, insistent bang came from the ceiling. It was so loud, he was sure some sort of demon dog was going to fall through and eat him whole.

It was time for level two of his "am I dreaming?" test. Jesse had developed a pretty reliable system, since he'd spent the majority of his life fearing sleep for the terrors it brought. Jesse took a tennis ball from his nightstand. He turned it around until he found his drawing of a single, cracked bowling pin. It was usually wrong or missing in dreams.

Jesse heard a low growl that sent shivers up his spine. If it was a hell hound, it probably weighed at least a ton to make a growl like that. Time for the second part of the second test. Jesse tossed the tennis ball across the room. It hit the wall and bounced off at the expected trajectory, bouncing back toward him along the floor until it rolled to a stop. In dreams, the ball always seemed to bounce strangely, catch in mid-air, get sucked into the wall, or something equally surreal.

The fact it had bounced normally meant he was almost certainly awake. Alarm grew deep within Jesse. A dusty fear of his ever-present nightmares coming to life bubbled up from the dark place in his mind where he'd locked it away long ago.

Click. The sound brought Jesse out of his thoughts and back into his room. He watched, eyes wide, as the knob on his bedroom door turned. The door creaked open as loudly as he'd ever heard it in real life. Jesse prayed to as many deities as he could remember, certain the Reaper himself was about to come through the door. But as it opened, he saw nothing.

At his wits' end, Jesse resorted to his third test. He opened his nightstand and took out the Bible he kept there - not for protection, but because of a trick a clever psychologist had told him in his teenage years. Jesse had seen plenty of psychologists growing up. Most attributed his dreams to anxiety or an unstable home life. None had been able to fix his dreams, though.

This psychologist had told him that the part of your brain you dream with isn't the same part that processes written language. So, if you try to read something in a dream, it will turn out to be gibberish. Out of the corner of his eye, Jesse watched a ceramic pencil cup slide across the top of his dresser and shatter as it hit the floor. He nearly ripped the Bible open. His fingers quivered as his eyes settled on Mark 9:21.

Jesus asked the boy's father, "How long has he been like this?" "From childhood," he answered.

Jesse didn't know what to do. This was real. Every moment of it. He almost wished he could just die and be done with it, but he worried for his soul. He was worried the thing scaring him might catch it and keep it to play with or eat it so it never reached Heaven.

Then, just as quickly as it had started, everything stopped. Jesse spent the rest of the night shaking, fading in and out of shallow, troubled sleep.

The next morning, Jesse hauled himself out of bed with a Herculean effort. He was still incredibly anxious from the night before, and his eyes felt puffy from insomnia.

On his way to his computer to check his email, like he did every morning, Jesse noticed something odd on his mantle. He wiped the sleep out of his eyes to make sure they weren't playing tricks on him, but sure as he stood there, a small porcelain cat lay there, tipped over with one of its front legs snapped. The cat wasn't his – he had never seen it before.

B.H. Werner

Cautiously, Jesse inched across the living room toward the cat. He slowly reached out to poke it with his finger, but then he drew back. Maybe he shouldn't touch it. What if it was an omen? Or some sort of cursed object? Was he the cat? Did something want to hurt him? He looked around until his eyes landed on the fire poker by his fireplace.

Jesse felt a little silly coming at an inch-and-a-half-tall porcelain cat with an iron spike, but he still didn't know where the cat had come from, and with the events of the past night, he wasn't taking any chances. Jesse tentatively extended his arm to poke the thing from as far away as he could. Nothing happened.

Jesse pushed it around a little bit. Still nothing. He put his hands on his hips and puffed out his chest.

"Is that all you've got, kitten?" he roared out, his confidence building, still feeling a little sleep deprived.

Satisfied that he wasn't in any immediate danger, he grabbed the porcelain feline and its leg and walked them out along the front sidewalk to the garbage. No more blank-eyed strays in his house today.

What did the delicate thing on his mantle mean, though? Jesse pondered a swirl of hazy possibilities between mocha sips and cornflake crunches. He was going to see a medium tonight anyway. Maybe it was dumb, but he wanted to try to tell his mother goodbye one last time. Maybe the medium could shed some light on the cat incident, too.

Jesse closed his car door and dumped his keys in his pocket three blocks from the fortuneteller's shop. He hadn't thought the neighborhood would be a problem, given that it was a prime shopping and dining destination, but evidently things got a little sketchy once you got out of the bright lights of the main drag. Jesse figured his car stood a better chance of not getting stolen on the main street.

The back streets were less glamorous. Trash clogged gutters. Signs sagged. Chipped paint flapped in the wind like dandelion seeds trying to fly off and find new homes. Jesse crossed the street to avoid a homeless man who was having a heated argument with someone who wasn't there.

Finally, Jesse saw the sign: "Lady Grarcic's Trinkets & Divinations." The sign in the window said "OPEN," so he pushed open the door and stepped inside. Hot, stuffy air and incense instantly hit him. The thick, plush carpeting was red and felt like it was laid over cheap floorboards. Crimson velvet curtains draped every doorway, tied back to the doorframe at waist height.

"Hello?" Jesse called out, not seeing the fortuneteller from the small front entry hall.

"Back here," a woman crowed in a slight foreign accent. Jesse followed the direction he thought he'd heard the response from, making his way through a series of small, garish rooms filled with trinkets and figurines.

"Marco," Jesse called out when he reached a dead end. The place was obviously a house or series of apartments at one time, now converted into the labyrinth-like shop.

"Polo," a voice called out, closer this time than before. Jesse rerouted himself toward the voice and found an older woman sitting at a small circular table covered with a vividly patterned cloth. She looked tired. Jesse hoped he was going to get his money's worth.

"What can I help you with today?" the woman asked, opening her arms in half-hearted gesture of welcome.

B.H. Werner

"It's my mother," Jesse said as he pulled out the wooden chair closest to him.

"Is she sick?" Lady Grarcic asked.

"Dead," Jesse replied.

"I'm afraid there's not much I can do about that," the woman said, her face tightening.

"I know that," Jesse said, a little annoyed. "I was hoping you could help me speak with her spirit. She died suddenly, and I didn't have a chance to say good-bye."

"Ah." The woman sighed in understanding, her face relaxing. "What was her name?"

"Doreen."

Lady Grarcic arranged several candles on the table and lit them with a cheap grill lighter. Evidently the spirit world wasn't picky about *every* detail of arcane rituals. "Lay your hands on mine," Lady Grarcic said, putting her palms up on the table. Jesse placed his hands on hers. He tried not to flinch. They were wrinkled and clammy. The medium closed her eyes.

"Do I need to close my eyes, too?" Jesse asked.

"No, just me. But you do need to remain quiet from now on unless I tell you that you can speak," Lady Grarcic warned. She began to chant quietly. Jesse couldn't make out any of what she was saying; it seemed to be in a foreign language. The lady swayed slightly, too. Jesse wondered if the medium would be able to reach his mother, or if she had been dead too long, or if it was all just a clever way to con him out of fifty bucks.

As his thoughts began to wander, Jesse saw a shadow pass over the table from behind him. It was as if someone had run across the room, blocking part of the light coming from the bright overhead fixture there. But there was no noise. Not a footstep. Not a shuffle.

Lady Grarcic's eyes flashed open in alarm. "What have you brought here?" she asked, as if he'd brought a wild panther.

"Nothing, I just want to speak with my mother," Jesse said.

The medium jerked her hands back. "Have you come here to destroy me?" she yelled, scooting back from the table and glaring at Jesse suspiciously.

"Destroy you? No, what's going on?" Jesse demanded.

"You've got evil on your back, son, gnawing on your mind!" Lady Grarcic shrieked, standing and shoving her chair behind her.

Jesse was shocked.

"Get out!" the lady demanded, pointing toward the door. "NOW!" she bellowed when Jesse hesitated. She swung around the table and hurried him through the shop. He was so surprised, he ran from her feeble hands slapping at his back. Jesse hopped the tall threshold out the front door, and it slammed behind him. He turned around to ask for an explanation, but the woman flipped the OPEN sign around to CLOSED and jerked the curtain over the window.

A series of clicks followed. Jesse didn't realize anybody had that many locks. Pissed off and even more confused than when he'd started, Jesse headed for his car.

Angry that he didn't get anything helpful out of the fortuneteller and frustrated that he felt like he knew less and less about his own mother, after work Jesse

B.H. Werner

decided to try and take down a small tree branch that had been tapping against his roofline for the past few weeks. Working on his yard always gave Jesse a sense of calm. He gloved up and then pulled a small chainsaw out of its bright orange case and made sure the fluids were at their proper levels.

Satisfied, he carried it outside and eyed the branch for a plan of attack. The branch wasn't too big, and the part over the roof didn't look very heavy. He decided he'd just cut it near the base and let it fall the seven to ten feet to the ground.

Then he spotted an orange neighborhood cat sitting defiantly in the middle of the branch. Remembering the mysterious porcelain cat on his mantle, Jesse wondered if it was some sort of prophetic message. A warning. A vision of the cat falling with the branch and breaking its leg swam around inside his head, and he pondered how to convince it to move before he started sawing.

Jesse started by yelling at it. It just curled up. Then he hissed at it. It watched him with a bored expression. He tossed a few small pebbles from the yard at the cat, and it meowed at him indignantly. He tossed a few more, and the cat decided it was a game, swatting at them like flies.

Jesse sighed. He was sure the noise from the chain-saw would scare the stubborn cat away. He primed the saw, then revved it a few times until it buzzed to life.

The cat started and took off to another branch. Jesse smiled and laid into the branch just past where it met the larger branch. The metal teeth cut into the wood and sawdust started flying.

About three quarters of the way through, the branch started to make a cracking sound, and the upper portion bowed to rest easily on the edge of Jesse's roof.

B.H. Werner

Jesse pulled out the saw to go at the last stretch from the underside of the branch.

But while he rested his saw, the incorrigible orange cat returned to the branch. Jesse tried shooing it again. The cat stared at him blankly. *Fine*, Jesse thought, his patience long gone, *you want to sit on that branch that badly? You can ride it all the way to the ground!*

Jesse revved the chainsaw, and a final push turned the branch loose. But instead of falling straight down, like he had anticipated, the branch took a funny angle and swung wildly on its way down. Jesse dropped to the ground to avoid getting hit, and his chainsaw sputtered out without his hand on the safety lever to keep it running.

He looked around for the cat, but he didn't see it at first. He got up to see where it had run off to. He heard a pained feline growl come from under the foliage of the downed branch.

Jesse mimicked the cat's sound to see if it would respond, and it yowled again, louder this time. It was definitely under the branch. Jesse carefully pulled the branch up, revealing the battered, angry cat. He tossed the branch aside and surveyed the animal. One of its front legs was bent at an odd angle.

Crap, he thought. He hadn't meant to hurt the stupid cat. Maybe just scare it a little for being such a pain. He ran back into the garage to get a strong cloth bag to gather the cat in. He wasn't just going to leave it there, injured as it was, but he knew hurt animals could be a handful.

He managed to get the cat into the bag with only a few dozen scratches and cinched it up before dropping it off at the vet. Diagnosis? Pissed off, with a broken leg.

B.H. Werner

His mind went to the porcelain cat on his mantle again. He didn't know what it meant, but it made him uneasy.

Despite being completely rattled about porcelain prophecies, Jesse had the best night of sleep his entire life that night. No disturbances. No dreams. Just peaceful, restful, glorious sleep.

Jesse slept wonderfully for three nights. It was more than he could have imagined. But on the fourth night, Jesse's real life nightmare struck again.

This time, it was less tentative. It didn't beat on the ceiling and open the door across the room. This time, it drug things off his night stand, threw his clothes at him, and shook his bed. This time it was showing him it could touch him if it wanted to. It could hurt him if it wanted to. Jesse cowered and waited for it to stop. Just as before, when he'd reached his wits' end and couldn't take any more, it stopped cold.

Jesse couldn't be bothered to cook the next morning. His mother dying had been plenty. Losing the closest thing he had to a friend at work had been too much. And the thing that was haunting him was almost more than he could bear. He wished he knew why it had come back. He'd give anything to have just a few more nights of peaceful rest. If there was a heaven, he was sure everyone there was sleeping soundly.

It was a Saturday, so Jesse went to his favorite breakfast spot. It was a small local diner staffed by girls with nose rings and guys with ironic beards, but they served some of the best pancakes in town. A table by the front door was covered in flyers for local events and neighborhood posters covered the walls.

As Jesse peered absently at the menu, pretending he was going to order anything but his usual, a poster over the table at his booth caught his eye. It was advocating against beating the homeless. "They're people, too," it said. Evidently, it was an epidemic. He hadn't heard much about it, but according to the poster, lack of awareness was part of the problem.

Even though he didn't care much about the cause, Jesse couldn't stop looking at the poster. He'd try to look away, but he'd always be drawn back to it. Some detail would grab his attention and pull his gaze.

"Hey, buddy, what can I getcha?" said a thirty-something guy with a pad, a white t-shirt, and ample sideburns that went all the way to his chin and connected with his mustache. He looked impatient. He must have already asked a few times.

Jesse absently ordered his regular and let his eyes drift back to the poster.

"Terrible stuff," the waiter said.

"The pancakes?" Jesse asked, confused.

"No, the beatings," the waiter replied. "Did you know ninety percent of all violence against the homeless goes unreported?"

"No, I didn't know that," Jesse said.

"Well, if you're interested, you should check this out." The waiter slid a brochure with artwork matching the poster onto Jesse's table.

"Thanks."

"No problem. Every bit of help counts."

The waiter left to tend to another table. Jesse opened the cheaply-printed brochure. The inside contained a map of attacks against the homeless. *If I was looking to beat up a hobo, this would be the perfect roadmap,* Jesse thought. Then something clicked.

The cat hadn't been an omen. It had been an instruction. The thing had made his life miserable until the porcelain cat showed up. Even though it hadn't been deliberate, he had broken the cat's leg. Once he had followed the clue, he had had three nights of perfectly good sleep. But that must not have been enough, or it wouldn't have come back last night.Now it wanted something more.

That's why it came after him last night. To make sure he was paying attention this morning. That's why he couldn't stop staring at the poster. That's why there was practically a roadmap to beating up hobos in his hands.Jesse paused at the thought of doing intentional violence. But then he remembered things flying across his room. And he remembered three nights of sinfully comfortable slumber. Maybe he could just kick a homeless person and run away, or shove them into a dumpster.

His pancakes arrived, and he tried to figure out which spot on the map he wanted to use. He shoveled his first bite of breakfast into his mouth. He felt syrup run down the side of his chin. Too big a bite. Jesse tried to wipe it, but before he could, a drop landed on the brochure. He wiped his face off with a napkin and was about to wipe the spot off the brochure until he saw that it had landed on the perfect spot for a nighttime ambush. Now he understood.

Map in hand, Jesse negotiated the pristine streets of the business district. If you didn't have a map like the one Jesse did, you might never know that the back alleys of the business district were home to hundreds of homeless. Jesse decided to make his trip at night, since the district was a buzzing hive of suits and wingtips during the day. At night, it was only host to a few workaholics and people hanging out for drinks after work.

Jesse took a hard right into the alley still marked on his map with a maple syrup stain. Partway down the alley, the building to his right receded, making room for a loading dock. To his left, a dumpster sat against the wall, which continued on for another twenty feet before it intersected with a perpendicular alley.

As Jesse passed the dumpster, he saw what he'd been looking for – a scraggly man in his 50s with sun-scorched, leathery skin snoring quietly, half buried in cardboard. It was brisk outside, but the weather hardly called for the three jackets and two pairs of pants the man was wearing.

Jesse flipped up the hood on his sweater to help avoid being identified if anyone showed up in the alley while he was executing his plan. Not entirely sure how to approach his first blow, he fell back on what he'd seen in movies. He raised his foot up, ready to give the hobo a solid stomp, when he heard men joking around at the end of the alleyway. He withdrew his foot and hustled back to the loading dock area, hoping they hadn't seen him.

As he listened more closely, he could tell they were young and drunk. Probably guys on the bottom of the food chain at some big firm who'd had to work late, blowing off steam by talking trash about their bosses over a few beers. Their conversation kept on, just as loud as when Jesse had first heard it, so he peered around the corner to see if they'd stopped at the end of the alley. They had.

The three men were taking turns telling some sort of work-related war stories, gesturing wildly as they talked. Two of them were wearing fashion t-shirts with fake tattoos and graffiti printed on them. The third was wearing a collared version of the same. All three were wearing designer jeans and flashy shoes. One of the ones in the t-shirts actually looked pretty well muscled.

Jesse began to think he might need to reschedule, but something in his mind twisted around and the situation came into a new light. Those guys were young, drunk and into themselves. And Jesse bet they wouldn't be the type who'd take kindly to someone messing up their clothes, especially some indigent defacing their wearable trophies of capitalism.

So Jesse slinked over to the dumpster and found a good-sized can of, well, something the consistency of refried beans and much worse smelling. He took it back over to the corner where the loading dock opened up, took aim, and flung his putrid projectile, ducking back around the corner as soon as he let it go.

He heard a splat. Then cursing. Jesse took his hood back down so he looked like a normal guy working on the loading dock. He ran out into the middle of the alley where the three drunken douches could see him and yelled out, "He's over here! The guy who threw that can is right over here!"

Jesse pointed behind the dumpster as the three drunkards passed him. Their shouting roused the old man, which worked out nicely, as it wouldn't have been so believable if the guy had still been asleep. They reached the dumpster and jumped the scraggly man, kicking and punching as Jesse slunk back to watch.

He probably should have been horrified, but with each stomp, thump, and dull slap, he only heard his bed creaking as he snuggled up for a night of dreamless, undisturbed sleep. Hopeful that he'd upheld his end of the deal, or whatever he had, with the thing that had been tormenting him, Jesse snuck out a different alley and onto the main street as sirens grew closer. *Hmmm... maybe that poster is doing some good after all,* he thought.

Over the ensuing months, Jesse picked up more and more clues and went on more and more missions. Each time, it escalated. It had started with accidentally breaking a cat's leg. It had jumped to convincing some meatheads to stomp a homeless guy. Before he knew it, he was pushing people down stairwells and getting people's feet stuck in escalators.

But that wasn't the part that stuck with Jesse. The part that stuck with him was that good things had actually started happening in his life. With all the extra sleep, he was much sharper and more efficient at work. It had earned him a promotion. His newly pleasant attitude had lured in some potential new friends, and Kent had started talking to him again. Jesse had even met a hot yoga instructor at the gym. Oh, and Jesse had *started going* to the gym.

Jesse woke up wondering what clues might await him. It had been a few days since his last "sleep aid." Padding through his house in new fuzzy slippers and a comfy robe, he shook his computer's mouse to wake it up so he could check his email. His computer wallpaper had been changed to an image of a road cyclist. Clue #1.

Jesse made a note, deleted a few spam emails, and headed for the kitchen to get his coffee. A bus pass for the #89 bus sat on his kitchen table on top of his stack of unopened mail. Jesse had never taken the #89 bus. Clue #2.

Jesse sipped on the steaming cup of coffee on his way into the living room. He hit the button on his remote to check the weather. The TV made a cheerful, pre-programmed noise as it flicked on. An ad for Big Ricky's Burgers and Wings came on. Jesse ignored it until it played three times in a row. Clue #3.

Jesse got back onto his computer and looked up the #89 route. Then he ran a map search for Big Ricky's. There was only one Big Ricky's on the #89 route. Bingo.

The bus stop was a suburban one, without too many people milling around. Big Ricky's was on a block catty-corner to the one where the bus stop stood. Jesse parked his car in the parking lot of an office building and shipping center across the street from the bus stop. The office building hadn't invested in any external security cameras. It was probably the same cost-cutting policy that got them into the dull white Anywhere, USA office park they were in. Lucky for Jesse, though. That was the first of three reasons he had chosen to park in the lot.

The second was that he thought it might be suspicious to drive up in a perfectly good car only to take the bus. Nobody around here took the bus unless they had to. Third, he wanted to make as clean an escape as possible. The parking lot where he dropped his car was visually shielded from the bus stop by a modest incline and a row of hedges. That meant he could run off under a believable pretense and remove himself from the scene before anyone could reliably identify him. And they wouldn't be able to ID his car, either.

Chill wind cut at Jesse's hands and face as he went a hundred or more yards out of his way to cross the street at the light. It was a cold, gusty day, but cloudless, with the midday sun high in the sky providing a modicum of warmth. It seemed to take forever to get to the bus stop. He'd forgotten how spread out everything was in this part of town.

It all looked perfectly close together speeding along at 50, but when you were actually standing in it, your sense of scale changed completely. You realized what seemed close in a car was actually all hundreds of yards apart. You'd think the people at the bus stop would feel safe with all the businesses and offices around, until you realized how far away they were, and that they were all partially blocked from view by rows upon rows of parked cars lined up like ramparts. But that suited Jesse fine. It was exactly what he needed.

He finally trudged his last few steps to the #89 stop and looked at his watch. Five minutes, if the bus was on time.

"It ain't gon' be here for a few minutes yet," said a strong-looking, middle-aged woman, the only other person waiting for the bus. She looked like she was a veteran of this stop. Jesse smiled generically and popped in his ear buds. That way he could still claim ignorance if the cyclist was yelling or ringing a bike horn.

He fiddled with his phone in that way people do since they've forgotten how to engage with other human beings without slick digital intermediaries. The woman didn't seem to mind. She just waited patiently, confidently, with her hands folded on her lap.

Thirty seconds 'till go time. Jesse saw the bus just past the stoplight coming up the road. He stepped closer to the curb, but left room for a bicycle to squeeze by. The woman stood up and adjusted her bag, content to wait in the marginal shelter of the bus stop.

Jesse turned his music off so he could hear the telltale hum of thin tires coming down the sidewalk. His ear caught them faintly at first, like a swarm of approaching bees. Then louder. Jesse started to worry the cyclist would get here before the bus, but the bus driver must have been in a hurry, because he was going fast enough he looked like he was going to overshoot the stop.

If it were a movie, the moment would have slowed down. But it wasn't. It all happened in a blink. Jesse stepped forward just as the cyclist came even with him. He heard the first part of a warning that the cyclist involuntarily aborted as he or she ran into Jesse and was thrown in front of the decelerating bus. Jesse heard a loud thud and the squealing of bus tires. The bicycle was still clanging down the curb as Jesse turned around to look with practiced surprise.

"Oh my god, what happened?" Jesse yelled as he ripped his ear buds out and shoved them in his jacket pocket.

"It hit him, the bus just hit him," wailed the woman. "He was going too fast, and the bus was going too fast, and he ran into you when you stepped up to the curb," she continued, looking around to try to figure out what to do next. "They were both just going too fast..."

"Call 9-1-1," Jesse said commandingly, grabbing the woman by the shoulders. "I'm gonna go get help." Jesse ran across the street and plowed through the hedges toward his car before the bus driver got out. It was a good run, and he was winded by the time he got there. Jesse jumped into his car, started the ignition, and was on his way before he even caught his breath.

Jesse hoped the cyclist would be all right. He thought he saw a helmet somewhere in the chaos. Either way, he was going to sleep well tonight.

B.H. Werner

As he wound through the back streets, Jesse thought about duvets. He had never really thought about duvets before. In fact, he had never really thought about bed being a comfortable place before. It had always been a place he'd wanted to escape as soon as the sun peeked up over the horizon.

But now that he knew what a good night's sleep felt like, Jesse could think of nothing but beds and bedding. At work, he shopped online for 600-thread-count pillow cases and fluffy comforters. At stores, he lusted after stay-cool pillows and king-sized mattresses using space foam technology. No wonder people liked sleeping in. He was finally one of them.

Jesse went so many days without a clue or a bump in the night that he began to wonder if the cyclist had survived. But that Saturday, he got up to find his TV already on, playing a workout infomercial. Thirty women on screen dressed in spandex were all doing sassy dance moves in unison to strengthen their cores and firm their glutes while the one in front narrated. Jesse hoped he didn't have to do something to someone in one of his girlfriend Sophie's yoga classes. He'd be a lot easier to identify to someone who already knew his face.

Waking up his computer to check his email, Jesse found that his wallpaper had been changed to a big juicy steak on a plate — knife and fork on either side. He looked back at the TV. He wasn't sure he liked the implication. Not liking where any of it was going, he decided to skip the gym for the day.

That night, Jesse woke up with his arms cold. He realized the top of his sheets had been pulled down from his shoulders to his waist. He tried to pull them back up, but they wouldn't budge. He thought perhaps they were stuck at the foot of the bed, so he gave them a good hard yank. Still nothing. This wasn't normal. Then his sheets started pulling down toward his feet on their own. He tried to hold them up, but they kept sliding steadily down. Cold night air bit at his legs.

Invisible claws jammed into Jesse's thighs. He screamed out in pain, grasping at his legs, unable to affect the sharp grip the thing had on him.

He drew a breath as he felt the claws retract, but cried out again as the thing drew its claws down his legs, opening up his skin and letting shallow red channels flow onto his perfectly white, Egyptian cotton sheets. He knew he had to stop the bleeding somehow. Maybe the towels in the bathroom.

But before he could get up, the rivulets of blood on his legs flared up in scalding flames. *This is the end*, Jesse thought, *it's going to take me*. He didn't even have the mental capacity left to try to put out the flames. He just watched them flame up like road flares, stinging like a million wasps attacking at once.

But Jesse was wrong again. As the flames fizzled out and the smell of burning flesh slithered into his nose, Jesse looked down to find the gashes in his legs cauterized. *It's not done with me,* Jesse thought. *I still have a chance*. With that thought, he passed out, the cold air now soothing his singed extremities.

The next morning, Jesse woke up with new resolve, and, surprisingly, no marks on his legs. He would not be dragged to hell for failing to give one of Sophie's students a hamstring injury or a broken ankle. He was ready to do whatever he had to do. Or he thought he was, until he reached the kitchen.

B.H. Werner

Jesse entered to find one of his large pots already boiling on the stove with something in it. He turned off the stove to get a better look. The bubbles dwindled to reveal an athletic-themed Barbie chopped to bits. Arms, legs, hands, feet– they'd all been cut off at the joints.

The Barbie was dressed in black yoga pants and a light blue sleeveless top — just the outfit Sophie always wore to teach her classes. Its eyes were brown like hers. It even had her hairdo. Jesse was pretty sure Barbie didn't make hair clips that small.

Jesse felt sick. He ran to the opposite kitchen counter to vomit in the sink. He couldn't do it. He couldn't believe it. The message was completely clear. The thing wanted him to chop up his girlfriend and eat her. Jesse wasn't a cannibal. He wasn't even a killer, as far as he knew. He had to figure something out. Maybe an exorcist, or a cleansing, or something. Anything. Anything but this.

Jesse raised his head and wiped his mouth. He had a new mission now. And this one was his own. He took a minute to brush his teeth and gargle some mouthwash before jumping on his computer. He was going to research every type of spiritual cleansing known to man. This was going to end. The thing had finally asked too much of him.

That night, Jesse spent an hour setting up his room before he went to bed. There were crosses, vials, candles, tinctures, crushed leaves, and every kind of bane and evil deterrent he'd been able to find. *Get through that,* he challenged, still fuming at the thought of the boiling pot from the morning.

Jesse soothed himself to sleep with visions of being some kind of spiritual warrior, finally confronting the thing that had been tormenting him and banishing it from his life.

B.H. Werner

Jesse woke up cold again. This time, his sheets weren't pulled down. They were wound up in a long rope, spiraled around him like an anaconda.

"You have no power here!" Jesse yelled, ready to spout the rebukes he'd practiced that afternoon. "I cast you ou- " Jesse's voice cut off as the blanket squeezed the air from him. His muscles hurt as it tightened around them with a force he could hardly process. He felt the sheet loosen momentarily and tried to rebuke the thing again.

"Leave, foul beast! You have no place here!" Jesse screamed hoarsely. He heard a low, amused, sinister laugh. Then the sheet tightened again, even tighter than before. Jesse thought he could feel some of his joints starting to dislocate. Stars began to dance around his vision from lack of oxygen. He struggled, but it squeezed tighter still.

Maybe I am cursed to do this, Jesse thought, and the sheet let loose. Air filled his aching lungs, and a new thought of Sophie begging for her life flowed into Jesse's head.

The sheet moved, keeping Jesse's arms pinned and firmly wrapping around his legs. It dragged him quickly from the bed onto the hardwood floor, which he hit with a thud. His head smacked against the door jamb and the carpet in the hall burned his bare skin as the sheet dragged him to the stairway.

At the top of the wooden stairs, it paused, as if for dramatic effect. Maybe it wanted to give Jesse a chance to change his mind. Maybe it wanted him to think about what was coming. Either way, it didn't matter. The sheet pulled at his legs again and dragged Jesse, face down. His face and body thudded and crunched against every step all the way down the staircase.

B.H. Werner

At the bottom of the stairs, the bed sheet loosened for good. Jesse lay on the floor with blood pouring from his mouth, tonguing his teeth to see if he'd lost any. He thought about Sophie. He wondered if she was worth all this. He hadn't even known her that long. It's not as if she were the only eligible yoga instructor in the city.

Jesse thought about his nice warm bed, and then his aching lungs and his broken face. It wasn't his turn to suffer anymore. He'd already endured more than his fair share. It was time to stop worrying about other people's suffering and start tending to his own.

Jesse went through the day in a haze, barely noticing that his wounds from the night before were again miraculously gone. Everything seemed far away. It was as if his own body was trying to block his senses from what he already knew he was going to do. Work passed uneventfully. He made a quick stop at a corner store for a protein bar that he ate, but didn't taste. Then it was off to the gym. He barely noticed himself sweating at his workout class. The instructor adjourned the class, and Jesse headed for the locker room to shower off. Sophie caught him before he got there.

"Hey, I got your text," she said cheerfully.

"My...huh?" Jesse mumbled, still not fully present.

"You said you were sorry you couldn't make it this weekend, but that you had tickets to this super exclusive art show in the meat packing district tonight," Sophie said, her ponytail bobbing with her excitement.

"Oh yeah, you still wanna go?" Jesse asked, realizing this was his cue.

"Of course! Let's both go shower off and get changed, and I'll meet you out front at your car?" Sophie asked sweetly.

B.H. Werner

"Sounds great," Jesse said. He forced a smile. If she weren't so excited about the "art show," she probably wouldn't have bought it.

In the shower, Jesse saw the steam, but he didn't feel the heat. He pulled on his clothes, but his skin felt numb. Men were cracking jokes right next to him, but they sounded like they were underwater.

After finishing in the locker room, Jesse pulled his car around the snowy street. Sophie ran out from the front of the gym and jumped in the car, shivering from the cold. Even though he couldn't feel the difference, Jesse blasted the car's heater for her. It was the least he could do.

Twenty minutes later, they arrived at a dimly lit street in the transitional meat packing district. It was a place where swanky town homes shouldered up to crumbling warehouses and business people in wood-trimmed luxury cars drove past hustlers and hookers.

Jesse jumped out, got Sophie's door for her, and led her toward the building he knew would be the last place she ever saw.

"Where is everybody?" Sophie asked. A good question. Jesse should have thought it out more. He'd have to improvise.

"We got here a little early," Jesse lied. "I got special V.I.P. tickets to meet the artist before the show."

"Oh, cool!" Sophie exclaimed. She took his arm, and they made their way through the unlocked door to the warehouse supposedly hosting the art show. They walked through a short brick hallway that opened up into a medium-sized room. The beast must have been busy. The entire thing was already set up. A huge, im-promptu cutting board was already waiting, with a big diagram of beef butchering on the wall next to it. A large metal drum rested on top of a large gas camp burner. The water in it was already boiling. A doorway at an angle on the opposite side of the room revealed only the edge of a dining table and a chair.

Sophie stopped, clearly realizing something was off. "Hey Jesse, are you sure we're in the right..." Sophie never finished the sentence. Jesse took a hammer hanging from a hook in the wall and cracked her in the back of the head with it. He quickly stripped her down and dumped her in the boiling water. When she splashed in, he got a whiff of spices. It had been pre-seasoned. How thoughtful.

Some time later, an oven timer dinged. After a bit of preparation, dinner was ready. He took a serving on the lone plate from the cooking room into the neighboring room that had been teasing him with a peek of the dining table.

There, Jesse found a large rectangular table with an exquisite place set at both ends – one for Jesse, and one with a photo of Jesse's sadistic father Walter nailed to the chair. Jesse sat down amazed, the photo of Walter beaming at Jesse like he'd never done in life. The thing seemed almost alive with pride.

As he sat at the table chewing on a flavorful sliver of thigh, Jesse wondered if he had become a version of his father. He wasn't sure. What he was sure of was that for the first time, he and his father were having a nice family dinner together. And for the first time, he felt like he and his father saw eye to eye.

B.H. Werner

Peace Meal

Wayne Basta

Diego Chang, first president of Earth, faced his host, Lord Jursan, leader of the Hora Empire. Arrayed around them stood their respective honor guards — human, Fromier, and Hora. No one spoke.

Chang's small, blue-feathered Fromier escort, Ambassador Ordar, had explained that for the Hora, silence was a sign of respect and strength, and it was how all meetings began. Chang could only agree that it took strength to stand tall and remain quiet while surrounded by monsters that had murdered millions of people. It helped knowing that behind him stood General Gary Chevalier, hero of Earth.

Long minutes passed; Chang had ample time to survey his enemy. It was the first time they had met in person, and the first time in history that a human had boarded a Hora warship by choice, instead of as a prisoner, slave, or meal.

Lord Jursan was by far the largest Hora Chang had ever seen. Towering to almost four meters, he had enough muscle mass that he resembled a mountain more than he did a sentient creature. His orange, scaly skin looked harder than rock.

Finally, Jursan let out a guttural bellow, followed by a long string of hisses, grunts, and growls. Chang had tried to learn the Hora language, but he had always struggled with Earth languages, much less alien ones. Fortunately, Ambassador Ordar began translating.

"Welcome, worthy adversaries of the mighty Hora. You have fought well and proven worthy of our attention. We come here to end hostilities."

Chang cleared his throat with a gulp before responding in a deep baritone that resonated through the room. "Thank you, honored Lord of the Hora. You do us great tribute by accepting us into your presence. We have enjoyed the contest of war between our peoples, but we agree that the time has come to end the battle. Both sides have proven their strength to the other."

As Ambassador Ordar translated, Chang felt like a hypocrite. Humanity had not enjoyed the war, and it had not been a fair fight. While Earth's ships had been technologically comparable to those of the Hora, they had had few warships at the start. The Hora assault had wiped out several colonies before reaching Earth. Millions had died.

But the Hora respected strength and warfare. General Chevalier had shown humanity's strength by repelling the beasts off Earth. Rumor even said that Chevalier had killed some of the Hora in hand-to-hand combat. The man's victories had given Earth's allies, the Fromier, the opportunity to open negotiations by acting the role of a weaker party speaking for their masters. Everyone knew this relationship to be false; the Fromier often worked as the galaxy's peacebrokers. But the illusion played well into the Hora view of the universe.

Lord Jursan spread his arms wide and spoke louder, making it hard for Chang to hear Ordar's translation. "We will now seal this peace with *Kro'min'Jar.*"

Wayne Basta

Chang had heard the Hora word before, but not even Ambassador Ordar was able to translate it. Chang knew only that it was a necessary part of concluding the peace treaty.

Another Hora, almost as large and powerful-looking as Jursan, stepped forward to stand beside the lord. He drew a cruel-looking blade. In his hands, it looked like a dagger, but in Chang's, he was sure it would be a large broadsword. Handing the blade to Jursan, the Hora stood firmly at attention.

Lord Jursan continued, "As our offering for the *Kro'min'Jar*, I pledge our greatest warrior, Groevell. He won many victories against the people of Earth. Now that we are at peace, there is no foe worthy of his skills."

Then, without warning, Jursan swung the sword in a blur, slitting Groevell's throat. Blackish blood bubbled out of the dying Hora's throat, but he remained on his feet for an unsettling amount of time. Chang could do nothing but stare at the sudden brutality of the unexpected execution.

What happened next was an even greater shock. When Groevell's body did finally fall to the ground, Jursan bent down and cut open his chest. With the sickening sounds of sawing through flesh and bone, Jursan cut out Groevell's heart.

Stepping forward, Lord Jursan extended the bloody heart to Chang, who immediately noticed how much the organ resembled a human heart. In the dark room, he almost thought he saw it beating in Jursan's hand.

What the hell just happened? Chang thought. Nothing Ordar had described had mentioned the Hora sacrificing one of their officers and cutting his heart out in front of everyone. It took all the willpower Chang had

Wayne Basta

to remain steady and not flinch as he looked at the heart. Not sure what to do now, he turned to look at Ordar.

The feathery Fromier cast his eyes downward, indicating that what he said next was not a translation. "Jursan is offering you the heart of his greatest warrior to feast upon. It is the traditional ending of warfare among the Hora."

Chang's stomach twisted, nausea overwhelming everything else he had been feeling. While he wasn't a strict vegetarian, he ate very little meat. The idea of eating raw flesh, especially from a sentient being, disgusted him.

It went unsaid by Ambassador Ordar, but Chang got the message that if he refused this offering, the peace process would likely be over. The Hora had given him safe conduct onto the ship, so he thought they might allow him and Chevalier to leave. But walking away would cause the resumption of a war Earth could not afford.

Pushing aside his doubts and his repulsion, Chang reached out and took the heart from Jursan, needing both of his hands to accommodate the organ. The giant Hora remained where he was, watching intently. Feasting, apparently, should be done immediately. With determination, Chang bit into the slick, warm, and bloody organ.

The small bite he managed to tear off tasted like all of the worst things Chang had ever eaten. As soon as it was in his mouth, his body tried to get him to spit it back out. The gag reflex almost overpowered him. With difficulty, Chang managed to get the bite down his throat.

Looking up, Chang fervently hoped that one bite would be enough to satisfy the Hora. Staring fixedly into Lord Jursan's eyes, Chang tried to mask his revulsion. The Hora must have been satisfied, because a servant came forward and took the heart from Chang and placed it onto a tray.

Relief washed over him. The task had been disgusting and disturbing. He would undoubtedly have nightmares about this for the rest of his life. But it was over.

Then Lord Jursan handed the giant dagger to Chang, hilt first. Unsure what to do, he took the blade. As soon as Jursan let go, the heavy blade fell to the floor, the hilt slipping from Chang's blood-soaked hands.

Embarrassed, and hoping he didn't look weak, Chang bent over and picked up the blade, struggling to hold it steady in his hands. Jursan and the other Hora gave no indication the drop bothered them. They only stood, staring expectantly at Chang.

Unsure what he was supposed to do, Chang turned again to Ambassador Ordar. Still casting his eyes downward, Ordar spoke. "The Hora have made their sacrifice to the peace process; now it is your turn."

Chang's confusion was quickly replaced by shock, and he was unable to stop himself from exclaiming, "What?!"

"They have offered you the heart of their greatest warrior. Now you shall do the same. Once that is done, Earth and the Hora will be at peace."

Realization slammed into Chang, even wiping out the nausea he still felt. Slowly, he looked up to Chevalier. The man's face was stoic, his eyes fixed staring forward, and his body locked as if at attention. But be-

Wayne Basta

traying that hard, military exterior, Chang could see his left eye twitching ever so slightly.

"I can't murder him!" Chang blurted out, unable to keep himself calm.

"If you do not, the war will resume. And instead of just looking for a good fight, the Hora will be looking to redeem their honor, because you ate the heart of their warrior, but refused the same offer to them," Ordar explained.

Chang looked at Chevalier and shook his head. "Then we'll fight them off. This is wrong. Peace is not worth this."

"Do it, Mr. President," Chevalier countered, speaking for the first time. "I have always been ready to give my life for the people of Earth. Better here and now, to save millions, than later while fighting a hopeless defense."

Damn that man, Chang thought. So noble. He was asking Chang to kill him. How could he do that? Kill the man who had saved Earth?

But he could see no alternative. Chevalier would save the planet again by sacrificing his life. His president would go down in history as a monster, but Earth would be safe. Was not one man's life worth the lives of millions?

He had never wanted to answer that question: were the lives of some soldiers expendable? Avoiding it had motivated his push for peace with the Hora. Many people wanted revenge — wanted to invade the Hora worlds. But Chang had wanted to avoid more senseless deaths.

As president, he had succeeded in brokering peace with a relentless enemy, a feat few had expected him to be able to accomplish. To clinch that victory, all he had to do was answer the question 'yes' — one soldier's life is expendable for the greater good. It was simple, but it was not easy.

With a nod to Chevalier, Chang closed his eyes, and then, speaking through Ordar, he said, "As Earth's sacrifice, we offer General Gary Chevalier. Hero of Earth. Savior of our people."

When Chang finished speaking, he lifted the heavy dagger. Chevalier snapped a salute. He then stuck his throat out while still standing at perfect attention. The salute almost made Chang drop the sword.

Instead, he forced himself to lift the heavy blade and swing it toward Chevalier's throat. He had never wielded a sword before, unless you counted toy ones when he had been a kid. Instead of sweeping through a graceful and deadly arc, as it had when Jursan had killed Groevell, the sword fell clumsily.

His swing lacked accuracy, and instead of precisely slitting Chevalier's throat, the blade sliced into his neck and shoulder with a sickening crunch. It fell more from the pull of the ship's artificial gravity than from Chang's swing. But it was enough to sever arteries.

The mighty warrior of Earth fell to the floor instantly. Unfortunately, Chevalier's death took much longer than the Hora's had. Minutes went by as Chang was forced to watch his hero struggle for a last few breaths on the floor of the Hora ship.

When Chevalier finally stopped convulsing, Chang bent down, struggling with the large sword. Cutting out Chevalier's heart proved to be exceptionally difficult. By the time he managed to get it out, the Hora blood on his hands had been washed away, replaced by dark red human blood.

Wayne Basta

Surprisingly, once Chang had made his decision, the fear and nausea had vanished. Handing the still warm heart of Chevalier to Jursan caused him no emotion. He watched Jursan swallow the heart in a single bite, feeling distant, as if he were watching a movie.

Jursan then spoke again, with Ordar translating. Chang found himself unable to concentrate on the words. He realized it was time for them to leave only when Ordar made a small gesture back toward the door.

Moving his body on autopilot, Chang turned and left the room. He had eaten the heart of a sentient being. He had killed a man he had held in reverence. He was covered in that man's blood.

His chest tightened and uncontrollable shivers started arcing through his body. The sickly sweet smell of blood overwhelmed his senses, and breathing became difficult. What had he done? He wasn't sure how, but he managed to make it back to the shuttle before expelling the contents of his stomach onto the deck.

But they had peace now. The people of Earth would be sad about Chevalier's death. But they would understand that their hero had made the sacrifice to save them. They would understand that and not push for a war to avenge Chevalier. Wouldn't they?

Wayne's first novel, *Aristeia: Revolutionary Right* is now available in both print and ebook on Amazon and coming soon to Nook, iBooks and other retailers. The sequel, *Aristeia: A Little Rebellion*, is coming soon from Grey Gecko Press.

Wayne Basta

Miss Tilly

Amy Theacasi

Tilly stood in the gallery. It seemed only minutes before that the halls had been alive with people, all potential buyers now gone. It was only eight thirty, and the showing didn't close until ten. Her paintings had not been selling as well as last year.

She looked over at the open bar in the corner. Carlos, the caterer, was trying to look busy cleaning invisible residue off the wine glasses.

She leaned her back against the wall and tilted her head to drain the champagne from her crystal flute. Stepping out of her stilettos, she pulled her blonde hair out of a loose up-do, and a cascade of curls fell softly around her shoulders.

Carlos was now drying an already-dry countertop. He had been acting nervous all night. Originally from Italy, he held deep-seated superstitions from his home town and always found a reason to be worried about something. Tilly had been using his catering company for her art shows for the past three years. She trusted him overall, though sometimes he was a little too opinionated, constantly preaching God's word to her—and all the while taking a little off the top from the cash register for himself and his workers.

She didn't really mind; it wasn't enough to matter, and it was nothing compared to her own remarkably checkered past. Tilly was not a particularly reverent woman, and she found it amusing: all these years preaching the Good Word, and look what had become of him.

Tonight, however, there had been no preaching. Carlos had been quiet and preoccupied. From the moment he had walked into the gallery and seen her new display of works, he had seemed uncomfortable. She found herself rolling her eyes, chalking it up to his superstitious religiosity. Although it had not occurred to her before, it made perfect sense that the paintings bothered him.

She walked barefoot across the tile to her office. "You can clean up now, Carlos. The party's over."

"Okay, Miss Tilly," he said quietly.

She paused for a moment at his response.

So out of character.

She continued on, shaking her head as she walked away. Usually, he would encourage her to stay open a little longer on a night like this. He really did seem to be in a hurry to get out of the gallery.

But at this point, she was too tired and disappointed to care. She just waved her hand. "Okay, thanks," she said. "I'll be in my office. Come get me when you're ready to go, so I can lock up behind you." She turned back to look at him once more, but he was already hurrying through the hallway to the kitchen at the far side of the gallery. She just shook her head and walked up the marble steps and down the long corridor to her office.

An hour later, Tilly was still sitting at her computer mulling over new ideas for her next series of paintings when she realized she had been hunched in the same position for too long. Sitting up straight, she leaned back in her chair, massaging her head with her fingertips. She swiveled her chair around to face the wall, which was was made entirely of glass, giving her a spectacular view of the gallery below. She liked to gaze out onto the marble tiles and majestic columns for inspiration.

She stood and squeezed her head between her palms, releasing the tension of the day as she walked toward the glass, but then she stopped short in the middle of the room. Her brows narrowed and she strained, focusing on the far side of the gallery where she had seen Carlos disappear toward the kitchen. She could see a figure standing perfectly still, just within the shadow of the doorway, facing her such that only the outline of his body was visible. She brought her hands down from her head and walked closer to get a better view.

"What's Carlos doing?" she said to herself, beginning to get impatient with the weird mood he was in. She waved at him and put her hands up in an exaggerated shrug as if to ask 'What's up?' No response. She exhaled in exasperation and spun around to walk out to the gallery, her impatience now turning to full-on annoyance. Her hand was on the doorknob when she stopped suddenly and pulled back.

She looked at the clock on her desk then down at her wristwatch. It had been well over an hour. It usually only took him and his staff forty-five minutes to clean up, and that was after a busy night. Turning her attention to the gallery again, she saw that the figure in the doorway downstairs was gone.

She looked down at her hand, suspended in the air inches away from the doorknob. It began to shake.

Tilly, this is ridiculous.

Amy Theacasi

She shook her head to gather herself, stood up straight and turned the doorknob, opening the door slowly to reveal the long corridor one inch at a time. It was empty. She took a couple of steps into the hallway before she looked up again, and then she gasped.

At the end of the corridor stood the same dark figure from downstairs.

"Carlos?" she called out. Her voice echoed back at her.

She could feel sweat beginning to seep through her pores, and her heart beat heavy and fast in her chest. Her breath quickened, and she swallowed hard.

"Carlos? Are you ready to lock up?" She laughed nervously. "Hey, what are you doing? Are you okay?" She took one step in his direction and froze. This was not Carlos, she could see that now. But there was something familiar about the figure, and she thought it so strange to be able to recognize anything about him in the darkness. And then it hit her. She felt the hair on the back of her neck stand up.

"It can't be," she whispered to herself.

He began to walk toward her.

As he came into the light, fear washed over her. It was unlike anything she had ever felt. It gripped her body, beginning with a heat that flushed her cheeks as the blood rushed to her head. The heat traveled down the back of her neck and tingled as it filled first her shoulders, then her arms and hands, covering her shaking palms with a thin, moist layer of sweat.

He was still walking toward her. The tingling wave of fear washed down to her stomach and then to her legs, paralyzing them.

Run! Run!

Amy Theacasi

Her eyes were wide; tears welled up and fell silently down her cheeks as the figure took on its true form before her eyes. Gasping for breath, Tilly shut her eyes and then opened them again, finding herself face-to-face with her enemy.

She gasped for the last time, and a scream formed deep in the pit of her gut, rushing out of her mouth and echoing throughout the empty gallery.

Detective Scotts squatted and leaned over the body, his trench coat gathered on the floor. The forensics team was finishing up.

"What have we got here?" he asked no one in particular. He was only thinking aloud, but an answer came from above his head.

"Well, sir, head's completely gone."

Scotts looked up at a short, chubby little man wearing slacks that looked about two sizes too big. He wore a faded polo shirt tucked in and a belt to cinch it all together, seemingly the only saving grace keeping his pants up.

"Hi. I'm Dr. Jay Rainer. I'm the pathologist on duty. I'd shake your hand but, well, you know." He held out his bloody gloved hands as if to show proof of the work he'd been doing on the body.

Scotts stood and grimaced at him, swiftly becoming annoyed.

Rainer didn't seem to notice. "This here is Miss Tilly Stone. We've been here a few hours, and we still can't find her head. Not sure what became of it," he said matter-of-factly. "Oh, and look at her back." He kneeled down and turned the body on its side to reveal a mess of shredded flesh, her entire spine revealed. "I'm not

Amy Theacasi

sure what sort of weapon did this. There is a lot of damage here, and it seems it was done while she was still alive."

"He was torturing her," Scotts thought aloud again. "Did you say you can't find her head?"

"Nope, looked everywhere. It's a small, private gallery—didn't take us long to cover it all. If you walk right down these steps to the other side of the gallery, there's another corridor leading to the kitchen."

Scotts was looking down at the body, taking notes and half listening to Rainer.

"That's where we found the rest of the bodies... in the deep freeze," Rainer said.

Scotts looked up from his note pad. "The rest of the bodies? Who else was here last night?"

"Oh, here, I'll show you," Rainer said. He looked past Scotts to one of his team members and said, "Finish up here while I take the detective downstairs." He walked down the corridor and motioned for Scotts to follow. "It seems she was showcasing her paintings last night, and she hired a catering service. The entire crew was thrown in the deep freezer. They froze to death," Rainer explained as they walked across the gallery, their voices echoing.

Scotts jotted notes as he walked, forming various scenarios in his mind. Little Miss Tilly had pissed someone off pretty bad. He wondered why they hadn't just waited for the staff to leave.

They walked into the kitchen, where another team was busy working up the bodies while a few officers stood watching.

"Here they are," Rainer said, as if he was showing Scott a prized car collection.

Amy Theacasi

Scotts took a moment to look at each body, then he looked up at Rainer. "Have you found where he came in?"

"Oh, that's another thing," Rainer said. "There's no sign of forced entry, and, well, we aren't really sure how he got out."

"Out... of the building?" Scotts asked, puzzled.

"Well, the cleaning crew came in this morning to do the usual dusting and polishing, but when they got here, they couldn't get in with their key, because the doors were locked from the inside. They got worried when they couldn't reach Stone on her cell phone, so they called the cops. Cops came, broke down the door, found this."

"Locked from the inside!" Scotts' annoyance with Rainer's demeanor quickly turned to anger. "He was probably still inside when the cops got here! Did anyone think of that?" He barked orders at the officers to lock up the doors and stand vigil, calling for backup and hurrying past Rainer at the same time.

Rainer stood stunned for almost a full minute while the thought of a murderer lurking in the building sank in. When he finally snapped out of it, he turned and ran to catch Scotts. He found him standing in the gallery, staring at the giant paintings on the wall.

Rainer nervously jogged over to him and asked, "What do we do now?"

Scotts ignored his question. "What's going on here?" he asked.

Rainer looked at the paintings for the first time and thought for a moment before recognition crossed his face.

Amy Theacasi

"Ah, yes," Rainer answered. "Don't you know your Italian literature?"

Scotts didn't move; he just stood there, staring at the paintings. "Refresh my memory," he said slowly.

Rainer seemed to forget his precarious situation once given the opportunity to show off his extensive knowledge on the subject.

"Oh, well, here you have Caïna, first ring or 'round' of the ninth circle of Hell. Are you familiar with the Divine Comedy, Mr. Scotts? Dante?"

Scotts remained perfectly still. "Remind me."

"Oh. Well, okay, she must have painted each round of the ninth circle. So this is round one, and over here you have rounds two, three, and four. Each round punishes a different set of sinners. Round one punishes those who sin against their kin. Round two, called Antenora, is for those who sin against their city or county, and round three, Ptolomaea I believe is the name, is reserved for those who sin against their guests." Walking along the wall of the gallery, he pointed to each painting as he spoke.

"Go on," Scotts mumbled, a pinched cigarette between his lips. He was struggling to strike a flame on his lighter.

Rainer pointed to another painting from the other side of the gallery, raising his voice to be heard. "This one here is Judecca, and from the name, you can probably guess that it's reserved for those who sin against their lords and benefactors... you can't smoke in here."

"I'm not," Scotts replied, a billow of smoke escaping as he spoke. "Keep talking."

Rainer began looking around the gallery. "There is one missing," he said. "The center of Hell should be here. It is reserved for the ultimate sinner who, of course, committed personal treachery against God himself." Rainer looked confused. "It must be here somewhere; otherwise, the work is not complete... I can't imagine she would..."

"It's over there," Scotts interrupted, his cigarette trailing smoke as he pointed.

Rainer noticed the other wall where the final painting hung. It had been hidden from his view by one of the marble columns.

"Oh, yes," he said, walking over to the painting. "Here we have..." He stopped. "Well, that's strange."

"Finish what you were saying," Scotts said.

"Well, it's just that it's so strange..."

"Finish it!" Scotts interrupted. "How does the story go?"

Confused by Scott's sudden need to understand the arts, Rainer went on. "Well, you see, the four rounds of the ninth circle are in contrast to the traditional view of Hell. In the poem, it is a very cold place." He motioned back to the four majestic paintings on the main wall, depicting traitors, their bodies contorted at various depths within the icy rings of Hell.

"See, they're all frozen," Rainer pointed out before looking back at the final painting. "Here, of course, is the center of Hell, where the ultimate sinner is condemned. In the poem, Dante finds him here, punishing Judas. He is described as gnawing on..." Rainer stopped in mid-sentence, fear silencing him.

Scotts had walked over to stand next to Rainer, and he was now at Rainer's side, finishing his sentence. "He is gnawing on his head and forever skinning his back," Scotts said.

Amy Theacasi

They stood staring at the final painting, realization tugging at their grip on reality. The one thing missing in the center of Satan's Hell was Satan himself.

Amy Theacasi

The Art of Steaming

Jason Kristopher

"Blast that prig, Fontague," Daniel muttered as he stood staring at the tunnel grate. The gas streetlamps barely threw any light his way; the cold London fog shrouded them in mist and a halo of light. "Blast him and Victoria, all of 'em. Let 'em come down here and fix these damnable pipes themselves. Wouldn't do for them to get their hands a bit dirty, though, would it?"

He kept muttering as he pulled the grate up, scraping it across the cobblestones of the street. He gathered up his bag and lantern and climbed down the ladder into the tunnels. Daniel hated the steam tunnels. He hated everything about London, though, so that was hardly a surprise.

What he hated most was the insufferable gentry, and especially Lord Fontague, who had him down here tonight fixing some old pipe or another when it would just break again in two or three days.

He lifted the lantern a little higher, trying to see down the tunnel, but couldn't make out where the leak was coming from. *There's nothing for it, Danny boy*, he thought. *You're going to have to go see for yourself.*

He shivered, despite the heat, and crept forward along the cobblestones, trying to whistle but only producing a strange, diseased sort of warble that he quickly put out of its misery. Left in the quiet, with only the hissing of the steam and the drip of the water, he resolved never to come back down here, Lord Fontague be damned.

Ah, there's the beastly leak, he thought, spying a steady stream of water spilling to the ground from a rusted-out pipe. He dropped his bag and pulled out a spanner and clamp, laying them next to the bag. Finding a convenient hook near another poorly-maintained pipe, he took advantage of it for the lantern.

The light barely reached the ladder, giving him just enough light to know his way out was still there. He had just picked up the spanner to get to work when he heard the noise.

Click, click, click.

He spun around, spanner in hand and ready to be used against whatever phantoms might be down here, but he saw nothing. Just as he had convinced himself it was, in fact, nothing, and merely the vagaries of the steam tunnels, he heard it again.

Click, click, click.

The steam was loud in his ears, but the blood pumping through his now-racing heart far exceeded that simple noise. He felt as though he were in the middle of a race; his vision narrowed, he smelled more of the awful detritus and noxious fumes that inhabited these tunnels... he could even hear the pings and creaks of the tunnel's metal access grate cooling in the frigid night air.

Click, click, click.

It was closer now, he was sure. *Danny boy, now is not the time to be a hero.*

He spun around, grabbing the clamp and bag, moving fast back toward the ladder to fresh air and freedom. Just as he noticed that he could barely see the ladder in the darkness, he realized he'd left the lantern behind on its hook.

Click, click, click.

He turned around, fearful to his core at what he'd see. At first, there was too much steam for him to see anything, but then the clouds of vapor parted slightly, and he saw a shadow cast by the lantern behind it.

Meaning, of course, that whatever was casting the shadow was now between him and the lantern.

It was a shadow unlike anything he'd ever seen. The creature clearly had two arms, two legs, what might've been a head... but the arms were *far* too long, nearly dragging on the ground, and the head was misshapen, elongated and nearly pointed.

Click, click, click.

He saw the long finger of the shadow's right hand tapping on the stones as it moved forward, tapping as if eager to reach its destination, impatient to slice and cut. Dropping all pretense, as well as his bag, Daniel ran for and scrambled up the ladder, reaching the refreshing London air and rolling to one side of the hole in the street. He quickly shoved the heavy metal grate back into place, and it thudded down into position just in time.

Click, click, click.

This time, the sound was muted, though it had a curious ringing quality to it, and it took only a moment for Daniel to realize that it was tapping on the ladder, now, rather than the stones. He moved back into the light of a streetlamp, carefully keeping an eye on the grate. When nothing disturbed the grate, he leaned against the wall behind him, catching his breath.

He felt as though he'd been stuck in those damned tunnels for hours and was only now able to breathe.

Jason Kristopher

The cold brick and marble wall at his back felt solid, real, as though it was the only real thing left. Taking deep draughts of the cold night air, he finally gathered his wits and stood, absent-mindedly brushing non-existent lint and dirt off of his clothes. Glancing around, he noticed that the street was empty.

Good job there's no one to see you, Danny, he thought. *No one to know how you ran.* He shook his head, trying to clear it, and stepped away from the wall, toward the street. *Maybe I can find a copper. There was definitely* something *down there.*

Sure enough, as he moved away from the grate and down the street toward the High Street intersection, he saw a bobby twirling his baton as he walked his beat. *Even coming my way*, he thought. *Fancy that. This'll be alright, after all.*

He flagged down the officer, who eyed him, staring down the beak of a nose Cyrano de Bergerac would've been proud of. Daniel hesitated for a moment.

He looks familiar, somehow, thought Daniel. *I know him from somewhere, but that's impossible. I don't know any bobbies.* With a mental shrug, Daniel let it go. *Who knows where I know him from? I just need him to listen.*

"What can I do for you, my son?" asked the officer, staring at him like the loon he felt he was. What's all this, then?"

"It's... well, there's something in the steam tunnel, sir." Daniel was nervous, trying to figure out how to explain what was going on without confirming that he was, in fact, a loon.

"Oh?"

"Yes, sir. Something nasty."

The officer snorted, crossing his arms. "Let me guess, a big lizard, right? Teeth the size o' me arm sort of fing?"

"Actually, no. Two arms, two legs, all the usual bits, but the arms are too long and the head is the wrong shape and..."

The officer held up a hand, stopping the tide of information pouring from Daniel. "Having me on, are you, sir? Monster in the tunnel? How much have you had to drink tonight, sir?"

"I'm *not* having you on, officer. I promise what I say is true; there is something down there, and it is *not* right!"

"I'll be the judge of that, my lad. Very well, show me this tunnel, then."

Daniel took the bobby over to the tunnel grate, and told him the story all over again, including how he'd leaned against the wall after climbing out. The officer's face was unreadable as he looked at the tunnel grate and glanced around.

"This wall over here?" the officer asked, pointing toward Daniel's resting place. When Daniel nodded, the officer moved to the wall, examining it closely while Daniel waited next to him.

Click, click, click. Click, click, click.

Daniel spun around, staring in horror at the tunnel grate as it began to turn in place, then to rise slowly.

"See, officer? What'd I tell yer? That noise..."

"That noise, sir, you never should have heard."

With what seemed to be a helplessly infinite slowness, Daniel turned back to the bobby, who had stepped back into the shadows of the alley next to the building. The officer seemed to be... changing, his arms lengthening, the outline of his head becoming more pointed as the bobby's helmet fell off.

"You're... you're..." Daniel couldn't speak, only stand there stunned as the transformation of the officer continued. He barely heard the scrape of the metal on cobbles as the steam tunnel grate slid aside. He was mesmerized, trying to see more and at the same time less of the creature he had thought was a policeman.

Even in his disbelief, Daniel finally recognized the man by virtue of the features he was rapidly losing. *Put him in a tie and tails, and I'd have picked him out right away,* Daniel thought. *It's Lord Fontague's butler!*

It was only when he finally heard the snuffling behind him, and felt the long, thin blade of the creature's finger tapping on his shoulder, that he thought of screaming.

The next evening, Lord Fontague sat back from the table in his well-appointed dining room, tossing his linen napkin negligently onto his now-empty plate before his manservant took the finished dish and headed for the kitchen.

"Well done, Nigel," he said, as he picked up his glass and drained the last of the delectable Spanish wine. "An excellent pairing."

"Thank you, sir."

"That was a very unusual cut of meat. How did Chef prepare it?"

Nigel turned back, the light from the large fireplace sharply outlining his face, including his overly large nose and long, thin features.

"It was steamed, sir."

Jason Kristopher

The Arrangement

George Wright Padgett

It had rained for days, and tonight was the worst of it. A vindictive storm pounded on the roof of the restaurant without reprieve. Sheets of rain ricocheted off the café, collecting in channels of water that were once streets.

A dark figure sat in the back of the restaurant alone, wearing a dark trench coat and a hat. The small candle on his table danced and flickered as he scanned the room. The hour was late, a few minutes to midnight by St. Louis time, and the restaurant was empty save for a few folks finishing their coffee near the front.

The patrons seemed too absorbed in their own story-telling, drunkenness, or both to notice him. Even so, he had arranged to be let in through the service door in the back to avoid any attention.

Across the dining room, a slender, dark-haired busboy lugged a large plastic container as he cleared all the tables. The half-empty glasses, plates, and silverware chinked and chimed with every step. He set the tub down and started flipping the wooden seats upside down onto all of the unoccupied tables.

After a few minutes, the room was a forest of inverted chairs with branches pointing to the low ceiling. The worker dutifully reclaimed his black container of dishes and retreated back through the aluminum doors.

For an instant, the cold fluorescent light of the kitchen escaped as the doors swung like pendulums.

Not much longer, thought the man in the corner.

Italian music seeped softly in through a small house speaker above his head. He didn't mind it. During the year and a half that had passed since his arrival, he had been exposed to various genres of the planet's music. As far as he was concerned, music was the only thing he had encountered of the culture that actually obeyed a set of rules.

He found himself listening to it, even enjoying figuring it out on some level. He was fascinated by the mathematics of the sounds' harmonic structure, creating atonal tension and resolving the dissonance continually like waves lapping the shoreline, a delectable panorama of rhythmic equations.

He caught himself staring at the plastic red-and-white checkered tablecloth and realized he was daydreaming. He chastened himself for letting his guard down. *I have to be more careful.*

"Good evening, Mr. Smith. Sorry to have kept you waiting. We are so glad you're here tonight," said a stocky man who was approaching the table while offering a smile that was too big to be sincere. The visitors always went by *Smith* or *Jones* or *Johnson* at these things.

"Mr. Smith," the man went on, "my name is Philippe. If you are ready, we may begin."

Smith nodded, attempting to mask his contempt for this man.

Philippe proffered a thin computer tablet.

Smith did not receive the device, leaving Philippe to suspend it awkwardly in the air.

George Wright Padgett

Is this a trap? They assured me this place had been checked out.

"Is... everything all right, Mr. Smith?" said the man as he tilted his head slightly and brandished an even larger smile.

"No paper? You don't use paper files here?" Smith scoffed. "I hate those tablet things."

"I see... I see. Is it because of leaving fingerprints? Because I could wipe-"

"No, it has nothing to do with that." Smith leaned in and spoke softly. "In this present condition — in *my* present condition, in this shell I'm occupying — I sometimes emit subtle electrical discharges that can short out devices like that."

Philippe withdrew the device and softly put it on the table between them. He took the seat across from Smith and scooted the chair in closer. The wooden chair legs made a short high-pitched bark as they scraped across the floor to their destination.

Philippe's round abdomen docked itself at the edge of the table as he said, "Mr. Smith, I apologize. The reason we don't print this type of information out is strictly that of discretion. Your associates have determined that paper can be reconstructed even after the most thorough shredding, but the files on this device are encrypted in such a way that over a million combinations have to be reconstituted to restore a single line of text."

The crooked smile reappeared. "So you see, once we are done, the subject will dissolve away as if it was never here."

Hmmph... In more ways than one, Smith thought. *In more ways than one, you opportunistic little man.*

George Wright Padgett

He studied the human for a moment. Smith wondered if Philippe, assuming that was his real name, thought that he would somehow be exempt when everything started up a few months from now. Did he really believe that clandestine meetings such as this would garner him favor when his species was being processed for elimination?

Selling out his own kind — how despicable. Are all humans like this greedy creature? If so, there is a certain justice to what is about to befall them.

Philippe continued, "The... *others* used this without any problem; in fact, it is on loan to me from your... eh... *friends.*"

"What are you saying?"

"The others, your..." Philippe struggled for an appropriate term. "Your colleagues, it did not present a problem for them." The man raised his palms and his eyebrows. "Not to worry, Mr. Smith. No worry. I will read the... uh... 'candidates' to you. I will read for you to decide, yes?"

Smith nodded again and crossed his arms.

Philippe reclaimed the pad and flicked it on. It chirped out an eager series of blips, the screen illuminating the operator's face. The man mumbled a pass code as his bloated fingers mashed the glass display.

Smith loathed coming to places like this, but this was about the only perk of being on an advance team. Certainly there were risks of doing it this way, but he liked having the control. By not going through some type of liaison, he'd be able to decide for himself what he wanted.

"Ah... there we go," said Philippe, angling the tablet's screen for Smith to view.

"First, there is Donna G. Cunningham: Caucasian, age 38; a housewife and mother of one from Ferguson." The light from the screen cast long shadows across Philippe's face, making him look like a grotesque caricature.

After a moment, Philippe asked, "No, *signor*? This is all right. I have many to choose from. Many more. Do not worry." His plump index finger tapped and scrolled the screen forward. "I just need to better understand the range of what you are looking for."

"No homeless, no children, elderly, or feeble... and no mentally unstable or physically ill. Understood?"

"Oh, of course not. Wouldn't dream of it, would not even begin to dream of it."

Smith remained unimpressed. He watched the man's over-enthusiastic manner each time a different profile appeared on the screen. Philippe reacted to every summary and picture as if it were some new discovery, forgotten until now.

"Now here's an interesting one: a 22-year-old aircraft mechanic; a Korean male from Manchester, Missouri named Daniel Yu."

"No, keep going," answered Smith. This was beginning to become tedious to him. As Philippe rattled through an assortment of races, ages, and vocations including a female SCUBA instructor, a city councilman accused of having an affair, a beverage distributor, a satellite TV installer, some joggers, and a meter reader, Smith began to wonder if he had made a mistake in coming here. This was going nowhere.

His mind drifted. He made a mental note to revisit this location in a few months, after the first offensive, of course, to see what had become of this place.

Maybe the Echelon will turn this place into a processing area, or just level the entire block to rubble. Either way, this self-serving parasite won't be here to see it. This realization made him smile.

Philippe picked up on the smile but misunderstood its meaning.

"So you like this one? This Michael Ackerman? It is a very good choice."

"Ackerman? Oh... tell me again, where is he from?" asked Smith, attempting to rejoin the conversation.

"Like I said, he is originally from Greendale but has recently returned from fighting in Uganda. Do you know where that is, Mr. Smith?"

Smith shot back sourly, "Yes, Philippe, I know all about Uganda. I am a *surveyor,* of sorts."

Philippe shrank in his chair. "I am sorry, Mr. Smith. I didn't mean to-"

"I know of places that you have never even heard of," interrupted Smith.

"I understand. I apologize again; truly sorry." Philippe avoided looking at Smith, choosing instead to stare at the tablet. "Ackerman, Michael... Serviceman Ackerman, recently returned from... Ugan- from combat. Two confirmed kills; age 31."

"Yes," Smith replied.

"Because of the extra difficulty in obtaining a specimen like..." Philippe stammered before taking a second pass at what he wanted to say. "You see, it costs more for someone like-"

"I said 'Yes.' I will take him."

Philippe peered up again. "Such a selection is well worth the extra amount of-"

Smith plopped a thick wad of cash upon the table so hard that the impact made the silverware bounce and clink against the bread dish. The excited flame of the candle flickered sporadically, leaping around in the small glass holder.

"Does that cover it?" asked Smith in a low, steady voice.

Philippe nodded and quickly shoved the bundled bills into his vest pocket. It didn't hide the bulge of bills, so he removed the vest and folded it into a ball in his arms. For the first time during the exchange, Philippe smiled an authentic smile. Smith noted that the man's true expression was even viler than the used-car-salesman smirk he had been offering up until now.

Smith grumbled, "Anything else?"

"Uh, no, *signor*." Philippe pushed back from the table and stood. He offered a slight bow. "Right away, Mr. Smith. Right away."

He backed away, turning around just a few paces before he reached the swinging doors of the kitchen.

Only seconds later, Philippe returned to the table, this time with an expression of embarrassment instead of a grin.

"The soldier, Philippe. I want the soldier!" snarled Smith.

Philippe nodded eagerly. "Ah... yes, very good, very good. I know you want the soldier. A splendid choice, but will you also be wanting an appetizer with the meal you've selected?"

George Wright Padgett

Afterword

Jason Kristopher

First, I want to thank my friend Jonathan Maberry for agreeing to write the foreword for this collection. His much-deserved success is an inspiration to all of us in this collection, and we're very grateful for his effort and time on our behalf.

There was a time when this short story collection would never have existed. Not all that long ago, in fact. But perhaps I'm getting ahead of myself.

I like to say I've always been a writer, and it's true. I've been writing since I first put pen to pad in 7th grade, most likely in math class. Horribly written, awful stuff.

But I kept writing, and now, more than twenty years later, not only have I published a novel, I've created a company that helps publish new and emerging authors like myself, and in a way that keeps them the center of the process, rather than the redheaded stepchild, as so much of the industry treats us.

This collection represents not only the great work of some very talented writers—and showcases just how much latent mental instability is inherent in the profession, no doubt—but also the big chance that the authors are taking.

Grey Gecko Press is not a traditional publisher. It's not one of the Big 6 worldwide publishing houses, and its funding budgets aren't in the millions or billions. It's a small press, run by and for authors, publishing great books, selling them worldwide to readers at affordable prices.

I think I can safely speak for the other authors featured in this collection when I say thank you for your purchase of this title. You've shown that you support the independent artists, the small presses . . . the little guys. And if you've done that, maybe you're willing to do just a little more?

Tell your friends, your family, and your coworkers about Grey Gecko Press. Tell them what we're trying to do. Encourage them to read, and to support new and emerging authors. Sign up for our free Advance Reader Program and receive all our new releases absolutely free.

Who knows? Maybe the junior high schooler jotting down his story instead of paying attention in class will be the next Jonathan Maberry, Stephen King, George R. R. Martin or J. K. Rowling. Your support could make all the difference.

Thank you once again for reading, and we hope you enjoyed your meal!

A Fancy Dinner Party

About the Authors

Gabrielle Alan

When not mulling over her latest obsession (A Song of Ice and Fire at the moment (Winter is coming!)), Gabrielle Alan spends her time reading (Surprise! An author that reads) and ballroom dancing (mostly swing). She also believes in a liberal application of parentheses (if you can't tell). *The Finger of Death* is her first published short story.

Wayne Basta

As a child, Wayne Basta was introduced to science fiction at a young age by his father. Growing up on Florida's space coast only served to fuel his imagination and love of space, science and adventure. Wayne currently lives in Houston with his wife, son and dog. He remains a fan of geek culture, board games, video games, fantasy, science fiction and all around silliness.

Leo King

Leo King patterns himself after a stage magician, presenting glitz and glamour in a beguiling ruse of misdirection. Crafting each word to draw your mind into the route he wants you to take, he waits until the opportune moment to spring the reveal upon you. It's how he defines himself as a writer — the journey may be what you truly enjoy, but the destination has to be equally enjoyable. Leo has just finished his first novel, a mystery/thriller set in 1990's New Orleans.

Jason Kristopher

Jason currently lives in Houston and enjoys reading, writing, movies, music (live and not), the Houston Astros (winning and not), singing karaoke and the Texas hill country, especially the vineyards. His first novel, *The Dying of the Light: End*, is a zombie apocalypse tale and the first in a trilogy, available now from Grey Gecko Press.

Lee Lackey

Lee Lackey has written short stories and planned out novels since he was sixteen. Throughout that time, he's learned one thing: writing takes the patience of a saint. Now in Houston, Texas, he has had five short stories published online or in print (two collaborative and three with Grey Gecko Press). He has recently finished his first novel and hopes to see it published this year.

Austin Malone

Austin Malone is not a flesh-eating alien, but a reputably human writer who lives in Houston with his (totally human, I swear) wife and daughter, and the requisite cat. *Hybrid* is his first published short story (Austin's, not the cat's), and he has work upcoming in the South African Horrorfest anthology, *Bloody Parchment*.

George Wright Padgett

George Wright Padgett has always had a passion for story-telling. Born in Houston, Texas, he grew up consuming a steady diet of science fiction and comic books. His time is divided between being a husband and father of two, jazz piano player, graphic artist, playwright, and painter. With what time that's left over, he writes science fiction, short stories, and the occasional mystery.

H. C. H. Ritz

H.C.H. Ritz is a writer and community theatre director who lives in Houston, Texas. She's married to a wonderful human being and has a tortoiseshell kitty named Roxy Underfoot. She writes science fiction, and she has never eaten a baby - not even once. *Being Bad* is her first published short story, and is set in the world of her upcoming novel *Lightbringers*, due out in 2012 from Grey Gecko Press.

Amy Theacasi

A young wife and mother of two (plus pets), Amy lives just outside Houston TX. When she's not at her engineering day job, she sometimes finds the time to write. *Miss Tilly* is her first published work, and she is working on a longer piece due out this fall from Grey Gecko.

B. H. Werner

B.H. Werner writes unhappy endings. He believes that decisions that appear black and white at a distance may turn out to be grey up close, and he's fascinated by the decisions people make when faced with nothing but bad options. Born and raised across Texas, B.H. Werner lives in Houston with his muse and a small, furry minion. He keeps two things handy at all times: the number of someone who would help him bury a body and a bludgeoning tool in case of zombies or overzealous evangelists.

A Fancy Dinner Party